TRAVELS WITH **GANNON & WYATT**

AUSTRALIA

PATTI WHEELER & KEITH HEMSTREET

GREENLEAF
BOOK GROUP PRESS

Published by Greenleaf Book Group Press
Austin, Texas
www.gbgpress.com

Distributed by Greenleaf Book Group

For ordering information or special discounts for bulk purchases, please contact Greenleaf Book Group at PO Box 91869, Austin, TX 78709, 512.891.6100.

Design and composition by Greenleaf Book Group
Cover design by Greenleaf Book Group
Cover images used under license from
©Shutterstock.com/Arun Sankaragal; ©Shutterstock.com/
ChameleonsEye; ©Shutterstock.com/andreashofmann7777;
©Shutterstock.com/ice_blue; ©Shutterstock.com/Rob Wilson
English/Aboriginal translation source: bininjkunwok.org.au

Publisher's Cataloging-in-Publication data is available.

Print ISBN: 978-1-62634-731-1

eBook ISBN: 978-1-62634-732-8

Part of the Tree Neutral® program, which offsets the number of trees consumed in the production and printing of this book by taking proactive steps, such as planting trees in direct proportion to the number of trees used: www.treeneutral.com.

TreeNeutral

Printed in the United States of America on acid-free paper

20 21 22 23 24 25   10 9 8 7 6 5 4 3 2 1

First Edition

This book is dedicated to the people and wildlife impacted by the Australian wildfires.

"Our land has a big story. Sometimes we tell a little bit at a time. Come and hear our stories, see our land. A little bit might stay in your hearts. If you want more, you come back."

—Jacob Nayinggul, Manilakarr clan

The meaning of Aboriginal:
"Ab" meaning "from" or "out of"
"origin" meaning "beginning" or "source"
"al" meaning "one belonging to"

Excerpted from *Dreamkeepers: A Spirit-Journey into Aboriginal Australia* by Harvey Arden

ENGLISH/ABORIGINAL LANGUAGE:
TRANSLATION OF COMMON PHRASES

There are several different Aboriginal languages, yet they all understand each other's dialect. The translations below are from the Kunwinjku language.

I want to speak Kunwinjku—Nga-djare nga-wokdi Kunwinjku

Can you teach me?—Ka-mak kan-bukkan?

Yes, that's fine, I can teach you—Yo ka-mak kaluk bukkan

Where is your camp?—Ngudda bale yi-reddi?

I'm sleeping on the north side—Ngaye kakbi nga-yo

Let's go—Karri-re.

That's it, see you/goodbye—Bonj bobo

Go away!—Yi-ray!

Come here!—Yim-ray!

Yes, that's good—Yoh ka-mak

I am going to the shop to get food—Nga-re shop man-me nga-mang

CONTENTS

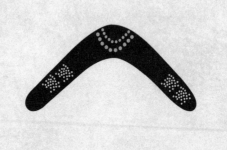

PART I

G'DAY FROM DOWN UNDER

GANNON

MARCH 9, EARLY MORNING
FLIGHT 892, SAN FRANCISCO, CALIFORNIA TO SYDNEY,
AUSTRALIA
MOOD: A LITTLE LOOPY

Australia might very well be the most *dangerous* country on the planet. And by dangerous, I mean *deadly*. And by deadly I mean that there are probably more creatures in Australia that can kill you than just about anywhere else on earth.

For starters, there's the inland taipan, the most venomous snake in the world; the eastern brown snake, the second most venomous; the box jellyfish, which is deadly; the Sydney funnel-web spider, also deadly; the stonefish, you guessed it, deadly; the textile cone snail, that's right, a deadly snail; and the cassowary, an ill-tempered, flightless bird about the size of an ostrich that can slice you open stem to stern with its razor sharp claw . . . so, yeah, pretty deadly. Not to mention enormous great white sharks and even more behemoth saltwater crocodiles.

So, here's a question. Do saltwater crocs actually swim in the ocean? Because that just sounds terrifying to me. I had to verify with Wyatt.

"Let's say I decide to take a dip at one of the beautiful beaches in northern Australia," I said to my twin brother. "Is it really possible that I could find myself sharing a wave with a crocodile?"

"A man-eating crocodile," Wyatt added. "That's more than three times your size."

"Wait, did you say *man-eating*?"

"Yes, I did."

"And did you say *three times my size*?"

"That's right. It's right here in the guide book: 'A saltwater crocodile can grow to be more than six meters in length.' That's almost twenty feet!"

Well, all righty then! I guess I'll scratch "Body surfing in Darwin" off my *Things To Do* list.

Of course, Australia is far better known for its long-tailed, bouncy marsupials, also called kangaroos (a word derived from an Aboriginal term, "gangurru") and the country's super cute and cuddly koala bears, but it's the less talked about creatures I listed prior that have me shaking in my coach seat, which, by the way, is in the very back of the plane, row 62, seat A, right next to the less-than-pleasant smelling bathroom. *Note to self:* Avoid at all costs the last-row, non-reclining, lavatory-adjacent seats, especially on 15-hour flights. Thing is, since my mom is a flight attendant at World Airlines and our family gets to fly for free, we usually have to go standby, which basically means we have to take whatever seats are still available, and the last available seats are almost always in the way back. But, hey, when you're getting something for free you can't really complain, can you? Of course you can't. And, at least it's a window seat, so I can take some video footage when we fly into Sydney.

Right, so where was I?

Oh yeah, pondering all the deadly things we might encounter while visiting Australia. Let me state for the record that I've traveled to some dangerous places in my day and learned how to survive in some of the most inhospitable environments on earth, so I'm pretty sure I'm up for the challenge. That said, a sensible person might ask the following question: "Why would anyone in their right mind want to explore a place with so many deadly creatures?"

Fair enough. The answer, though, is pretty simple. I mean, it's Australia! Home to the Great Barrier Reef, the Outback and the oldest living culture in the world! It's the Land Down Under! We're talking wombats, wallabys, and kookaburras! A country where people greet you with "G'day mate!" and say things like "Crikey!" Heck, I'd be crazy to pass up the chance to explore such an awesome place!

Earlier in the flight, about the time we crossed the International Date Line—which is this totally imaginary north-south line in the Pacific Ocean where it's a day earlier to the east of the line and already tomorrow to the west—Wyatt removed a map of Australia from his backpack and spread it over our tray tables. I turned on the overhead lights and together we spent some time studying the country's geography.

Most of Australia's major cities dot the eastern coast. There's Cairns, Brisbane, Sydney, which is the most populated city, and Canberra, the nation's capital. Very near the furthest point south on the mainland is Melbourne, the second most populated city, and smack dab in the dusty, red center of the country is Alice Springs, a popular base camp for those exploring the desert. In the far north sits Darwin, which is big-bad croc country, and last but not least, Perth, a lone metropolis on the relatively remote and sparsely populated western coast.

Tasmania, a small heart-shaped island with tall mountains and beautiful beaches, rests just off the southeastern tip of the Australian mainland. It's home to the infamous Tasmanian devil, an endangered and feisty marsupial that's about the size of a small dog, only with fangs that are closer to those of a wolf.

The wild terrain of the Australian interior, known as the Outback, has lured explorers for centuries. It's also home to the largest population of Aboriginal people. So, naturally, the Outback is where we're headed. One of my goals during this expedition is to spend time with Australia's first people, to listen to their stories and learn about their beliefs, especially their Dreamtime and songlines, which is their belief that they are continually singing the world into existence. My hope is that our experience will help me see life through their eyes, and if I'm lucky, gain some understanding of their ancient wisdom. Oh, and if someone can teach me how to play the didgeridoo while we're there, that would be totally awesome.

Whoa, look at that!

Through the window right now I am seeing the coastline of Australia for the first time! Funny, between all the reading I've done, the movie I watched, the journaling, and card games with Wyatt, this very long flight has actually zipped by pretty quick. I probably slept four or five hours, too, which helped. When I woke, the flight attendants were serving breakfast—a tasty cheese omelet, diced potatoes, vanilla yogurt, a fruit cup, and a biscuit. After breakfast, I put my books into the overhead bin, brushed my teeth, and just like that, here we are, making our final approach.

Oh, man, is this exciting or what? I'm guessing the rolling, misty hills to the west are the Blue Mountains. I remember them from the map. And, yep, I can see it now, off in the distance, the city of Sydney! Wow, check out all those tall buildings and sparkling blue waterways and little boats with their tiny white sails! And there's the Harbour Bridge, and oh my gosh, look at that . . . the Sydney Opera House!

Okay, you know what, time to put away the journal, grab my video camera, and take some footage of our arrival.

Signing out for now, but much more soon . . .

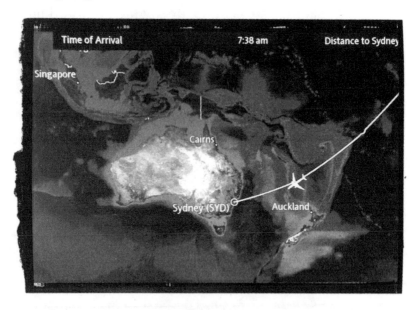

Map showing airplane's approach to Sydney.

WYATT

MARCH 9, 4:02 PM
SYDNEY, AUSTRALIA   33° 51' S   151° 12' E
81° FAHRENHEIT, 27° CELSIUS
WIND: 5-10 MPH
SKIES: BLUE

Sydney, in my view, is one of the most beautiful cities in the world. This is due mostly to its location on the water and two iconic structures, the Harbour Bridge and Sydney Opera House. The city's downtown area is safe and clean, with a number of parks, museums, restaurants, and pedestrian malls. Look up in any direction and your view is dominated by modern high-rise office buildings and condominiums. The quiet coves and inlets are inhabited by dozens of sailboats, all of them rocking back and forth in the choppy waters.

Setting off from the hotel this morning, my parents, Gannon, and I walked down to Circular Quay, a busy port in Sydney Harbour where passenger ferries arrive and depart. Meandering past the Writers Walk I noticed a series of plaques on the ground inscribed with the names of several famous authors, including Jack London and James A. Michener, two of my mom's favorites. From there, we made our way out to the eggshell half-domes of the Sydney Opera House and had a look inside. The interior is easily as impressive as the exterior, with high wooden beams, balconies, and rows and rows of seating.

"I can't imagine there are many performing arts centers that are more spectacular than this," my mom said.

The world famous Sydney Opera House

Following the waterfront away from the opera house, we came to the Royal Botanic Garden, a sweeping public haven of greenery. All through the park there are people riding bikes, jogging along the paths, or just lying on the grass under the sun, some reading, some conversing, and some even napping.

While my family continues to stroll the gardens, I have taken a seat on a bench next to a pair of snow-white cockatoos to write in my journal and reflect on how we came to be in this beautiful city, half way around the world from our home in Colorado.

About two months ago, my mom was assigned the San Francisco-Sydney route for World Airlines. It's a route she's always wanted to fly, and since we can hop aboard any time there are available seats, Gannon and I went right to work planning our own Australian adventure. I spent the better part of the next month reading everything I could find on the Land Down Under, making notes as I did to help us plan our expedition. This country is so big it's impossible to see it all, so we had some choices to make. What intrigued me most wasn't just the number of unique animals that exist in Australia today, but all the bizarre prehistoric creatures that roamed the continent tens of thousands of years ago. In a lot of ways, Australia is like a real life Jurassic Park.

With an itinerary in mind, Gannon and I wrote to the Youth Exploration Society and asked if it would be possible to meet with a Y.E.S. member in Darwin who could lead us on an exploration of the Outback. Soon after, we received a reply from an Aboriginal guide named Darla, who kindly offered to take us on a tour of Kakadu National Park. The "Top End" as it's also known, is the lush and rugged Australian bush I've always dreamt about. While there we will hike to the ancient dwelling places of the Aboriginal people, learn how they lived off the land, visit cave painting sites that date back thousands of years, and take a boat tour on the East Alligator River. According to Darla, we may even get a chance to cage dive with a crocodile in Darwin. Whether Gannon and I will actually have the courage to accept the offer is still up for debate.

My mission is to take comprehensive field notes on the climate and wildlife in the Outback, both present and pre-historic, while Gannon focuses his attention on the Aboriginal way of life. I was excited to learn that Darla is currently working with a crew of paleontologists who had recently uncovered a fossil of a Megalania, which was a venomous, meat-eating lizard that roamed sections of Australia some 30,000+ years ago. They looked a lot like a Komodo dragon, only they were twice the size.

"The Megalania," I read aloud to Gannon before we left, "was a land-based lizard that could outrun a human being and would grow to more than twenty feet."

"Just imagine what life was like for the first Australians," Gannon said. "You're sitting around the fire, having a nice chat, and a Megalania walks into camp and eats one of your friends!"

"That was just one of the monsters they had to worry about," I said. "Back then, every day was a battle for survival."

"Hey, maybe we'll find some fossils of our own while we're there," Gannon suggested.

"What if we find a Diprotodon?" I asked, excited by the prospect.

"I don't even know what that is," Gannon said. "But it sounds cool." "Only the largest marsupial ever! It looked kind of like a buck-toothed bear, but it was as big as a rhino!"

"Whoa."

"Or, maybe we'll discover a Procoptodon?"

"Don't know what that is either," Gannon said.

"Just the biggest kangaroo to ever hop the earth. Seven feet tall and more than five hundred pounds!"

"Man, that's one big roo! Hey, what if we found a new species no one has ever discovered before? Wouldn't that be so awesome?"

May seem far-fetched, but fact is, when you're on an expedition in the Outback anything is possible.

Tomorrow, after Gannon and I catch a plane to Darwin, my dad is flying to Uluru, a monolithic rock in central Australia, also known as Ayers Rock. While there, he will learn about the unique dot painting technique used by Aboriginal artists and will also make a number of paintings himself, mostly landscape paintings of Uluru at different times of day. According to my dad, who makes his living as a painter and a sculptor, the position of the sun, the light in the sky, and the clouds constantly alter the color and appearance of the rock. I'm sure his paintings will be impressive, but to be perfectly honest, the process of making them sounds awfully boring to me. No offense to my dad, but I just don't know that I could sit still hour after hour, day after day, watching a rock change color while delicately applying paint to a canvas. That said, I am excited to see the sacred rock myself when we meet my parents after our expedition.

My mom is catching a plane to Alice Springs in the morning where she'll get the opportunity to work with Aboriginal children at a school just outside of town. She told us that she has more to learn from the Aboriginal people then they could ever learn from her, so her plan is to simply assist the teachers however she can, and hopefully, to make some new friends in the process.

As part of our homeschool curriculum, my mom encouraged us to read up on two of the most famous explorations in Australian history—the expedition of Burke and Wills and that of the Prussian scientist, Ludwig Leichhardt, who was known as the "Prince of Explorers." I was somewhat unnerved to learn that the lives of these brave men all ended in tragedy, as our itinerary takes us over much of the same territory these explorers once trekked. Leichhardt, in fact, vanished in the Outback, never to be seen or heard from again.

Even though we have done our homework and are quite prepared, I can't help but wonder: might we encounter the same hardships as these famous explorers, the same fate? Not a pleasant thought to ponder, to say the least.

After exploring Kakadu, we'll hop a bush plane to a koala preserve, spend some time searching for fossils, then jump in a safari jeep and drive further south through the Australian desert all the way to Uluru, where we'll meet back up with our parents.

Setting my nerves aside, I honestly don't know that our itinerary could be better. Start to finish, this expedition is going to be action packed!

GANNON

MARCH 10
WALKABOUT IN SYDNEY

"Jet lag is catching up with me, mate," I said to Wyatt over breakfast. "I'm a bit knackered, but what do ya say we finish our brekky and go mucking around the city?"

I'd been working on my Aussie accent all morning. Personally, I felt like I was nailing it. My brother didn't seem to think so.

"Please stop with the Australian accent," Wyatt said. "It's getting real old, real quick."

"Oh, come on, mate," I said, laying it on extra thick. "You know I'm all about learning the local language. And since most people in Sydney speak English, I thought it'd be fun to use some Aussie expressions and work on their pronunciation while I'm at it."

"I hate to break it to you," Wyatt said, "but your accent doesn't sound Australian at all."

"Ah, bugger off, mate. My accent's bloody spot on."

"Mom, dad, would you like to weigh in?" Wyatt asked.

"Sorry, Gannon, but your brother's right," my dad said. "You kind of sound like someone who's just had serious dental work done."

"Right, and the Novocain hasn't worn off," Wyatt added.

I dismissed them with a wave of the hand.

"What do you think, Mom?" I asked.

"No comment," my mom said, and took another sip of tea.

My dad and brother laughed.

I chuckled myself, but wasn't about to give up.

"Well, we best get a move on, mate," I said to Wyatt, putting the video camera strap over my neck. "Let's go walkabout and find that safari outfitter we read about. If I remember correctly, it's a good ten clicks away."

"How do Australians say, 'Shut your trap?'" Wyatt said, his face crimson with frustration.

"Okay, fine," I said with a smile. "I'll give it a rest. For now."

Wyatt checked the settings on his camera, zipped it into his backpack and took one last bite of toast with jam. I stood from the table and slung my backpack over my shoulder. It was time to explore Sydney!

"Mom, Dad, we'll meet you back at the hotel later," Wyatt said. "We're going to a store called Outback Jack's to get some gear. According to the guide book, if Jack's doesn't have it, you don't need it."

"Sounds good, boys," my dad said.

"Stay together, be safe, and have fun," my mom added.

"We'll be back to our room before dark," I said.

"Brilliant, mates," my mom said with a big smile.

"Oh, no. Not you, too," Wyatt said, and smacked his forehead.

"Actually, Mom, that wasn't half bad," I said. "Sounded a little more New Zealand than Australian to me, but not half bad."

Wyatt rolled his eyes and walked off.

We really didn't have a mapped out route to Outback Jack's. It was more or less a random wandering, up and down hills, along crowded sidewalks packed with people, through beautiful parks and past fountains and monuments carved from marble, like the soaring statue of the famous sea captain and explorer, Captain James Cook.

Monument to Captain James Cook

Since we found ourselves in the area, we made a quick detour to zip up a small and very crowded elevator to the tippy-top of the needle-like Sydney Tower. At 1,014 feet, it is the tallest building in the city. The observation deck has floor to ceiling windows that offer a spectacular 360° view. I stepped to the window, leaned my head against the glass and looked down at all the people on the sidewalks below. It was such a cool perspective to take in the city from such a height. Everyone looked like ants. Then, out of nowhere, I was hit with this crazy wave of vertigo or something and suddenly felt like I was about to fall through the glass. With wobbly legs, I backed away from the window and took hold of a railing to catch my balance. The worst of the dizziness soon faded, but I was still a little unsteady and ready to be back on solid ground, so Wyatt and I caught the next elevator down.

Another mile or so away, tucked into a small storefront on Pitt Street, we found Outback Jack's. Walking into the store was like being transported into the Australian bush. There was a mock campsite with a canvas tent, chairs, and a fire pit, fake eucalyptus trees, and fake, but very lifelike, Outback animals in all these wild, menacing poses—a dingo, python, Tasmanian devil, all with their fangs exposed. From the speakers came the natural sounds of a rainforest.

"G'day, mates!" came a booming voice. "Welcome to Outback Jack's! I'd be Jack. Owner, proprietor, and skilled outdoorsman who grew up in the bush but moved to the city for the love of a beautiful woman. So, what can I do you for?"

I could tell right off, Jack was a character. A big, burly gent with a scraggly reddish beard, he was decked head to toe in beige safari gear. Atop his head was a leather hat, weathered and stained from years of wear and tear. The band that circled the base of his hat was decorated with an impressive set of big, white teeth. Crocodile teeth, I assumed.

"We're here to be outfitted for an Australian expedition," I said.

"Well, you're in the right place, mates," Jack said. "What specifically are you looking for?"

"A set of pants and shirts for each of us, a couple regional maps, and maybe a few other survival items for our backpacks."

"Where you headed, if you don't mind me asking?"

"Tomorrow morning we fly to Darwin," Wyatt answered. "Then on to Kakadu, Alice Springs, and finally, Uluru."

"Oh, good on ya, mates! Those are some wild places. The real Australia. I sure do wish I could tag along. You're in for quite an adventure."

"You know, Jack," I said. "I am really digging that hat you're wearing."

"This here's an Akubra," Jack said, removing his hat to show us. "I highly recommend you have one before setting off into the bush. That's harsh territory up there. An Akubra will come in handy, no doubt."

"Well, I'm sold," I said.

"Me too," Wyatt added.

"We'll take two please, Jack. And if you have one with crocodile teeth around the band, just like yours, that's all me."

"Sure thing, mate!" Jack said with a chuckle. "Let me pull a couple outfits that might work for you boys and then I'll grab the Akubras."

Jack made his way into the middle of the store and went about flipping through a rack of safari clothes.

Hanging on the wall among a section of nautical gear, was a framed photograph of a young girl standing on the bow of a sailboat.

"Who's that?" I asked, pointing at the photo.

"Oh, that there is Jessica Watson," Jack said, still going through the clothes. "One of Australia's greatest explorers."

Outback Jack went on to tell us that at the age of 16, Jessica Watson became one of the youngest people to sail solo around the world. During her unbelievable voyage, her boat, *The Pink Lady*, capsized six times. But Jessica didn't give up; she persevered. After 210 days alone at sea, she completed her journey, sailing into Sydney Harbour, where more than 100,000 people had gathered to greet her. It's one of the most inspiring stories of exploration I've ever heard. And to do it at 16 years of age, I mean, it's just unreal!

Over in the safari section were photos of Australia's usual suspects—crocs, roos, koalas, snakes, and so forth. What caught Wyatt's eye, however, was a picture of a creepy crawler that looked like a giant crab.

"What is that thing?" Wyatt asked, pointing to the photo.

"That bloke there is a spider, mate."

"Is that its actual size?" I asked.

"Sure is!"

"Can't be," Wyatt said, not wanting to believe it.

"It's a huntsman spider, largest in the world when you

measure it in diameter. They can be as big around as a dinner plate!"

"A dinner plate," Wyatt said, his eyes opening almost as wide.

"Didn't know about the huntsman, huh, Wyatt?" I asked.

"I intentionally skipped the spider section in the guide book."

"Are there any huntsman in the Northern Territory?" I asked Jack.

"Loads of 'em!" Jack answered with a laugh.

Wyatt seemed a little woozy.

"Toughen up, bro. I mean, look at Jessica Watson here," I said, pointing to her photo. "She sailed around the world, all by herself, and you're scared of a spider? That's pretty weak. Maybe you should stay in Sydney where you'll be safe and I'll tackle the Outback on my own."

"Shut it, Gannon. It's just . . . well, you know how I feel about spiders, and that thing is especially gigantic. I'd rather not see one during our expedition is all I'm saying."

"Maybe you won't," Jack said, and pulled a couple beige safari outfits off the rack. "If you keep your eyes closed!"

Oh, man, did I love that Jack had joined me in teasing my brother.

"What do you say, mates?" Jack asked. "Shorts or pants?"

"I'll go with shorts," I said. "I like to keep the old get-up sticks nice and cool, if you know what I'm saying."

"I'll take pants, please," Wyatt said.

"And how about shirts? Short sleeve or long?"

"Long again, please," Wyatt said.

"You're going to suffocate out there, Wyatt," I said.

"I want coverage, head to toe."

"Suit yourself," I said. "Jack, I'll take the short sleeve, please."

"Okay, try these on for size," Jack said. "Dressing rooms are right behind ya."

When Wyatt and I stepped out in our safari outfits Jack was waiting with two Akubras, both made of dark brown leather, Wyatt's with a black strap and mine with a set of polished white croc choppers, as requested. Jack set them atop our heads and stepped back to take a look.

"Lookin' sharp, mates," Jack said with a grin. "Lookin' real sharp."

"I have to say, I'm feeling pretty darn good in this outfit," I remarked, checking myself out in the mirror.

"Me too," Wyatt said, adjusting his Akubra.

Moving back through the store, we grabbed maps of Kakadu and Uluru, some waterproof matches, a multi-tool survival knife, two whistles, and a first aid kit and piled it all at the register.

"One more thing, mates," Jack said. "The flies out there are enough to drive a bloke mad. You may want a fly net to put over those Akubras."

"Are they biting flies?" I asked.

"No, just the annoying kind."

"As long as they don't bite, I think I'll be fine," I said.

Truth is, I was down to the last of my allowance and didn't want to spend an extra five dollars Australian on a net. Besides, how bad can they really be?

"I'll take one, Jack," Wyatt said. "Just in case."

We paid up, loaded our gear into our backpacks, put our Akubras back atop our heads and made for the door.

"G'day, Jack," I said, turning around to tip my hat. "And many thanks to ya."

"G'day, mates!" Jack shouted. "It's been a pleasure. Happy travels to the both of you."

On our way back to the hotel we ducked into a pharmacy and inquired about snake and spider anti-venom, you know, so in the event one of us is bitten, we don't die. Turns out anti-venom isn't something anyone can just buy and carry around in their backpack. We need a medical license or something, and obviously, we don't have one. The pharmacist told us not to worry, that anti-venom is kept at all the hospitals and clinics so they can treat people who have been bitten. Here's the thing: isn't it too late at that point? I mean, especially if you're in the remote Outback, hours from the nearest clinic. How could they possibly get it to you in time? Ugh, you know what? Let's just shelf this thought for now, otherwise I'll totally start to freak myself out.

Right, so, Wyatt just came back to the room and said we're meeting our parents at a nearby restaurant known for having the tastiest meat pies in all of Sydney, and since I worked up a solid sweat earlier and stink like a wombat after a rugby match, I'm going to put away my journal and take a speedy shower.

Okay, then. More tomorrow from Darwin, Northern Territory!

The view from Sydney Tower

WYATT

MARCH 11, 2:07 PM
DARWIN, NORTHERN TERRITORY   12° 27' S   130° 50' E
94° FAHRENHEIT, 34° CELSIUS
HUMIDITY: 92%
SKIES: PARTLY CLOUDY

We met our guide Darla at a small office on Mitchell Street. The windows were open and there was no air conditioning, despite the intense heat. A rusty rotating metal fan was the only device for cooling the room.

"Let me guess," Darla said with a welcoming smile as we stepped through the door. She pointed at Gannon. "You're Gannon, which would make you Wyatt."

"How did you know?" Gannon said.

"Last night I looked at your field notes and photographs in the Y.E.S. archive," she said. "I see that you've been all over the world."

"That's right," I said, proudly, but immediately wished my response had sounded slightly more humble.

"But you've never been to the Australian Outback."

"No, we haven't."

"It is an environment unlike any other, extraordinary and beautiful, but it can also be very dangerous." Darla paused to make eye contact with each of us. "Do you feel that you're prepared?"

Gannon and I looked at one another.

"We think so, yes," I said, wiping sweat from my forehead.

Again, Darla looked us over, her eyes penetrating and serious. Then a smile spread across her face.

"Well, you've certainly dressed for the occasion," she said, referring, of course, to our safari outfits.

"Courtesy of Outback Jack's in Sydney," Gannon said.

He took off his Akubra and spun around like a runway model, giving Darla a good laugh.

Darla is 18 years old, has curly black hair, brown eyes and a big, friendly smile that makes you want to smile right back at her. She grew up in nearby Arnhem Land, home to the traditional landowners, the Yolngu people. Her parents taught her how to live off the land from an early age, which makes her quite capable of surviving in the Outback. To build on an already impressive body of knowledge, she is studying environmental science in Darwin and guiding tours with her older brother in Kakadu. His name is Roman.

"Would you like to take a quick tour of Darwin?" Darla asked. "I'd be happy to show you around. This city has an interesting history."

"We'd love a tour," Gannon said.

We left our backpacks in the office bunk room where we will stay the night, filled our canteens with cold water, and set out onto the streets. The sun was fierce and I was completely drenched with sweat before we had even walked a few blocks.

Parliament House, Darwin, Northern Territory

Darla led us along Mitchell Street, a busy avenue lined with expedition companies, souvenir shops, restaurants and cafes. Professionally dressed business people and government workers moved quickly from one air-conditioned building to the next, hoping to avoid breaking a sweat. Casually dressed backpackers from all over the world sauntered down the sidewalks, seemingly without a destination in mind. Locals in shorts and t-shirts representing a wide range of ages and nationalities exited cafes, cold drinks in hand. Others sat quietly in the shade.

"Darwin is a multicultural city," Darla explained. "It is a wonderful mix of European, Asian, and Aboriginal lifestyles."

Darla went on to explain that Darwin's original inhabitants were the Larrakia Aboriginal people (there are many different Aboriginal groups in Australia). Europeans began moving to the area in the 1700s to establish ports and trading routes with Asia. Named in 1839 after the famous naturalist, Charles Darwin, this settlement at the top end of Australia is still an important port for international trade and has grown into a thriving city with a number of highrise buildings overlooking the water.

At the end of Mitchell Street we passed a jewelry store selling Australian white pearls before taking a right onto Smith Street. Darla pointed out the beautiful Darwin Public Library and the ruins of Palmerston Town Hall, which was destroyed by a cyclone.

"In 1974, Cyclone Tracy came ashore with wind speeds of two-hundred and fifty kilometers per hour."

"How many miles per hour is that?" Gannon asked.

"About one hundred and sixty," I answered, having done a quick calculation in my head.

"It was the largest natural disaster in Australian history," Darla told us.

To see the town hall, or what's left of it, just two crumbling stone walls, gave us an idea of just how powerful a cyclone can be.

The streets were canopied by magnolia trees and lush mangrove vines. A colorful rainbow lorrikeet squawked from a high perch. We continued over a pedestrian bridge that led to the waterfront, where people swam laps and kids played on inflatable slides anchored in the middle of a sheltered cove. This small area is walled off from the rest of the Beagle Gulf to protect people from sharks, crocodiles, and box jellyfish, making it the only safe place to swim in Darwin. Next to the cove was a large wave pool, where kids and adults alike splashed around in the crystal clear water. There were even a few teenagers surfing the pool's waves.

Having already drained our canteens, we stepped into a café for another cold drink, then took a short walk to the World War II tunnels.

"In 1942, during World War II, Darwin was bombed by the Japanese," Darla explained. "Two hundred and thirty-six people were killed. These tunnels were built by the military to store fuel and other important supplies for the Allied forces. Inside the tunnels the supplies would be safe from another air raid."

Exploring the dark, narrow tunnels carved deep into the rocky bluff, I imagined how difficult it must have been to live in Darwin at that time, under constant fear of being bombed.

Leaving the tunnels, we climbed back up the steep bluff through a dense canopied jungle, passing the Northern Territory Supreme Court and Parliament buildings, before pausing for a moment at the Government House, a white cottage overlooking the bay with manicured lawns and a white picket fence. This is home to the Administrator of the Northern Territory.

The local swimming hole offers protection from predators

Gannon stopped to fan out his shirt. His face was flushed, his hair wet and matted to his forehead.

"Is it this hot and humid year round or do you have seasons here?" Gannon asked, wiping sweat from his face.

"It's a little cooler and less humid in the winter," Darla explained. "According to Aboriginal wisdom, Northern Australia has six seasons."

"Six? What are they?" I asked.

"Gudjewg, Banggerreng, Yegge, Wurrgeng, Gurrung, and Gunumeleng. Right now we're in Gudjewg, monsoon season, but we're nearing Banggerreng, knock 'em down season.

They call it that because of all the wind, thunder, and lightning."

Gannon shook his head.

"I'm sorry, could you repeat all that? I lost you at Gudjewg."

Darla laughed.

"Tonight I'll write it all down for you."

"Thanks, Darla. That'd be great."

As we walked back through Bicentennial Park, Gannon filled the hot Darwin air with more of his own, posing question after question to Darla.

"Do you ever get nervous in the Outback?" was one that I was actually curious to hear the answer to. "You know, given that there are so many things out there that can kill you?"

"We do need to be careful," she said, "but do I get nervous? No, not really. I love anything that slithers, crawls, gallops, swims, or hops! That's why I guide tours. The Outback wilderness is a very special place and the more we teach young people about it, the more likely it is that they will take care of it in the future."

"That's a great mission, Darla," I said.

"Thank you," she replied, bowing slightly.

"You know," Gannon blurted, "while I'm on the topic of nerves, your letter mentioned something about swimming with crocs, which sounds totally insane to me. Is that really something you can do in Darwin?"

"Sure is," Darla said, her face lighting up. "In fact, the

crocodile rehabilitation facility is just a few blocks away. It's where we bring sick and injured crocs to be cared for. We can go right now, if you'd like."

I could tell Gannon wished he'd never brought it up.

"Oh, well, you know, we don't have to," he stammered. "I was just curious. Besides, I'm sure you have lots to do before we go to Kakadu and all."

"Don't be silly, Gannon," Darla said, putting her hand on my brother's shoulder. "I have all afternoon to prepare. It will be a wonderful learning experience that's totally unique to Darwin. Not many people get to swim with a giant croc and live to tell about it, right? Trust me, it'll be great fun. Let's go!"

Darla picked up her pace. We lagged a little behind.

"You had to bring that up, didn't you?" I whispered to Gannon.

"I'm sorry. I don't know what I was thinking."

"Obviously, you *weren't* thinking."

Everywhere we go my brother's big mouth lands us in uncomfortable situations. As I write, Darla is off speaking with some of the trainers to see if she can arrange a swim. We're waiting in the café next door. Gannon is seated beside me, nervously biting his nails. I had worked up an appetite during our walk, but I've lost it. Fact is, the last thing I care to do is swim with a crocodile. I just can't bring myself to admit that to Darla. I don't want her to think I'm a coward. Maybe there will be a reason we can't do it. Maybe the crocs are napping or the cage is broken or there's an approaching lightning storm that will keep us out of the water.

I'll be perfectly honest; any one of these things would make me a very happy guy. Okay, looks like we're about to find out. Here comes Darla . . .

GANNON

MARCH 12, MIDDAY
DARWIN, AUSTRALIA

Chewy, a really big saltwater croc!

Chewy is a 20-foot crocodile. I'm not exaggerating. Nose to the tip of the tail, he's 20-feet, with big, nasty teeth, a devious smile, and an aggressive disposition. He lost an eye and his front foot in a fight, and would have died if the people at the rehabilitation center hadn't nursed him back to health.

"Are you sure we should do this, Darla?" I asked.

"Like I said, where else in the world can you swim with a croc? You have to do it, right?"

I was guessing she was right, but I couldn't help second-guessing myself. I mean, true, it is a once in a lifetime opportunity, but also true is the fact that should the cage somehow malfunction and we were to fall into open water, Chewy would swallow us whole.

Here's the thing, even though Wyatt and I had only just met Darla, she was one of those people you felt like you'd known for years. She's easy to talk to and her enthusiasm for the "Top End" and all its wild creatures is plain to see. And I love all that, I do, but I couldn't help but feel like she was putting us to the test, making sure we were brave enough to tackle the Outback.

"Okay, gentlemen," Darla said. "You ready?"

"Absolutely," I replied, but my brave tone was nothing more than an act. Truth is, I wasn't ready at all.

"How about you, Wyatt?" she asked.

"I think so," Wyatt said.

"Excellent. Right this way to the Cage of Death."

I turned to Wyatt and whispered, "Cage of Death?"

Wyatt gave an anxious huff and reluctantly followed behind Darla.

At the cage, we were introduced to a trainer with long, blond hair, brown eyes, and tanned skin. She wore what you'd imagine a croc trainer might wear, a khaki golf shirt and cargo shorts, tan boots, and a safari hat. She told us to call her "Sky."

Being a trainer at the Darwin Crocodile Rehabilitation Center basically means that it's your job to feed the crocs (they mostly eat chicken and fish), give them medicine when they need it, keep their habitat clean, and educate visitors.

After watching a feeding, I concluded that being a croc trainer has to be one of the most dangerous jobs on the planet! They literally stand within a few feet of the croc while it lunges at them to snap up its food. I'm telling you, it's terrifying just to watch.

Sky led us to the cage.

"Not to be a pain in the butt or anything," I said, "but is there any chance you can give us a *personal guarantee* that this cylinder will definitely, without fail, I'm talking 100% certainty, protect us from being eaten alive? If we could get something like that in writing, I'd feel a little better about this."

"You're safe as can be in there," Sky said, giggling. "Just look how thick the glass is." She rapped on it with her knuckles. "Not even a croc can get through that."

"Okay, one more thing. If it's so safe, why don't they call it something more reassuring, like the Cage of Safety or the Cage of Safety?"

"Because Cage of Death sounds a lot bloody scarier, doesn't it?" Sky said with a wide smile.

Wyatt responded with a nervous, and I must say, very nerdy laugh.

"It will be fine, guys," Sky said. "Trust me. We haven't lost anyone yet."

"Yet?" I said. "The word *yet* implies that you're expecting to lose someone eventually, and that's what worries me."

Darla and Sky both laughed.

"We're not going to lose anyone, ever," Sky said. "You're overthinking this. Just get on with it. It'll be a real treat."

"For us or for Chewy?"

Again, the girls laughed aloud.

Okay, I'll admit, I had totally lost my cool. If Darla was, in fact, testing our bravery, I was failing miserably.

As the girls' laughter subsided, another croc trainer walked up to us, a tall and lanky guy with shaggy brown hair. It was curious to me just how young these trainers were. Sky looked like she might be 18, maybe 19 at most. And this guy didn't look much older than Sky. I couldn't help but wonder what their parents think about this risky career choice of theirs. I mean, I can't imagine they're thrilled that each day their children have to feed a 20-foot man-eater.

"Gannon, Wyatt, this is Dave," Sky said, introducing us to the male trainer. "He'll get you squared away in the cage."

"G'day, mates!" Dave said with a toothy smile. "So, you ready to join Chewy for a swim?"

"Um, I guess so," I said, with reservation.

"Can I take my underwater camera with me?" Wyatt asked, his voice a little shaky.

"Absolutely, mate."

When Dave opened the door to the cage, I noticed that he only had three fingers on his right hand—his pinkie, ring, and middle.

"I hope you aren't offended by this question," I said, sheepishly, "but do you mind if I ask what happened to your fingers?"

"That big bloke down there ate 'em!" Dave said, pointing at Chewy with his crooked middle finger. "It was my own fault. I was late feeding him. Chewy was a bit ticked, I got too close, and *BOOM*—he shot up at me like a missile, snapped up the chicken and two of me digits!"

"Jeez, I'm so sorry."

"No worries, mate. Could have been a lot worse. Besides, I can still use my other hand to hitchhike."

Dave stuck out the thumb of his good hand and acted like he was trying to catch a ride. Seemed odd to me that the story of losing a couple fingers would be funny to Dave, but I admired him for maintaining a sense of humor about it.

"What do you say we get you two in the water?" Dave asked. "Chewy looks lonely."

It was go time!

Lonely Chewy . . . or is it hungry Chewy?

After Wyatt sealed his camera inside a waterproof casing, we tossed aside our shirts and boots and climbed into the plexiglass cage. The cylinder-shaped enclosure was attached by several chains and a cable to a crane arm and conveyor, which lifts the cage and lowers it into the pool. Dave handed us each a mask, then closed and locked the door. I double-checked to make sure the lock was secure, pushing on the door hard with both hands.

"You're all packed away nice and safe!" Dave assured me. "Ready to take the plunge now, mates?"

We both nodded nervously and gave Dave the thumbs up. At our signal, Dave flipped a switch and the crane lifted the Cage of Death into the air and moved us over the pool. When I looked down into the water, I saw Chewy stretched out underneath us like a giant serpent.

"Why are we doing this again?" I asked Wyatt.

"Because Darla said it's a once in a lifetime opportunity and we didn't want to look like a couple of wimps," he said.

"Oh, yeah."

The Cage of Death entered the pool. Water poured inside, rising to about chest height before our descent stopped. Chewy was circling the cage at a distance of about 10 feet. I heard Dave yell, "Go on, Chewy! Give 'em a kiss!"

To entice the big croc, he attached a headless chicken carcass to the end of a long stick and dangled it over the water, a few inches from the cage.

"Got your camera ready?" I asked. Wyatt nodded timidly.

"Good, because here comes Chewy."

Wyatt and I both pulled scuba masks over our faces and sank below the surface. Underwater, the glass was virtually invisible, making it feel like we were floating unprotected in the pool. The water was clear, warm, and tasted a little gamey when it touched my lips. The pink flesh of a raw chicken bobbed up and down in front of our faces. Chewy floated ever closer. To tell the truth, at this point, I was kind of grossed out. I mean, swimming in a pool with a dead chicken and a wild croc who goes to the bathroom when and where he pleases can't be the most hygienic experience. But that thought was scared right out of my head when Chewy shot toward us with his mouth wide open! I jumped backward just as his jaw snapped shut like a bear trap against the glass. I might have screamed. I can't really remember.

Through the glass, I could see Darla and Sky standing on the observation deck, buckled over in laughter.

"That was intense," Wyatt gasped, as he came to the surface.

"No joke," I said. "Did you at least get a good picture?"

"I was so scared I dropped my camera."

"That's very professional of you."

Wyatt sunk under water to retrieve his camera, then came back up.

"I'll get the shot this time," he said, and took a few quick, deep breaths. "All right, ready to go back under?"

"I think so."

Sinking back underwater, I got a real good look at Chewy. He was so close I could have pet ted him, that is, if it weren't for the lifesaving plexiglass between us. Dave was still dangling the chicken over the water, yanking it away from Chewy every time he snapped at it. The tactic only seemed to aggravate Chewy, which is understandable. I mean, if someone was dangling a piece of pizza over my mouth and pulling it away every time I tried to take a bite, I'd get pretty upset, too. Eventually, though, Chewy grew tired of being toyed with. In a sudden burst, he whipped his tail, shot several feet into the air, and closed his powerful jaws over the chicken— *SNAP!*

I watched the wrinkly white skin under his mouth ripple as he swallowed the chicken whole. It was nothing more than an appetizer for Chewy, and a small one at that. Like me eating a popcorn shrimp or something.

After his snack, Chewy circled our cage. Observing him from underwater, I noticed that his left eye, green and gold speckled with a black slit for a pupil, was turned to the side. He was staring right at me. What could he be thinking? I wondered. If I had to guess, I bet he was wishing we'd join him in the water so he could have a proper meal. Cage or no cage, it sent chills down my spine to know that a croc had me in its sights.

Wyatt took a few more pictures and then our time was up. Apparently, some other nutcase wanted a turn. The crane lifted the cage out of the water and I took off my mask. Wyatt did the same. When we looked at each other, we both gave a sigh of relief. The Cage of Death had been a unique and thrilling experience, but also super intimidating, and to be totally honest, I was glad it was over.

We thanked Dave and Sky for keeping us safe and walked with Darla back to the expedition office in the sweltering afternoon heat. Inside the small courtyard was an outdoor shower that Wyatt and I used to rinse off the gamey croc water. Afterward, we changed into some dry clothes, hung our safari pants to dry and sat in the shade with our journals, eating fruit and drinking iced tea.

Our day in Darwin has been memorable, for sure, but

in the spirit of adventure, we're setting off at first light to Kakadu National Park, where we'll connect with Darla's older brother, Roman, and begin our expedition.

AUSTRALIAN OUTBACK, here we come!

Feeding time at the Cage of Death!

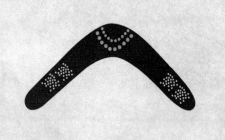

PART II

MAYDAY FROM THE OUTBACK!

WYATT

MARCH 13, 6:42 PM
KAKADU NATIONAL PARK, 12° 48' S 132° 44' E
79° FAHRENHEIT, 26° CELSIUS

Earlier today, Darla, Roman, Gannon, and I took a boat tour of the East Alligator River, which forms a natural border between Kakadu and Arnhem Land. The cruise began around 2:30 p.m. Dense forests and rocky cliffs crowded the banks. The air was thick with humidity. The sound of insects drifted over the water. In the trees we saw cockatoos by the dozens, egrets, ducks, and even a sea eagle on a high perch.

The river itself was calm and held a reflection of the cliffs and trees. If I didn't know what might be lurking beneath, I might have mistaken it for a nice place to take a swim.

"Hey, Wyatt, you going to wear that fly net or not?" Gannon asked, swatting at the flies that circled his face. "Because I'd be happy to put it to use."

I had completely forgotten that I'd bought one at Outback Jack's.

"Thanks for reminding me," I said, and retrieved it from my bag. "These flies are really starting to *bug* me."

"Ha-ha, hilarious pun, bro," Gannon said, his tone ripe with sarcasm.

I draped the net over the brim of my Akubra, pulled it down around my face and smiled at my brother. He glared back with envy.

"Ah, so much better," I said. "You really should have grabbed one of these."

"I would've if . . . " but his excuse was cut short when a bug flew down his throat.

He gagged, coughed, and spit several times into the river.

"Oh, gosh," he gurgled. "I just swallowed a fly!" Gannon's hands shot up to his neck. "Ugh, yuck, I can feel it flapping around in my windpipe!"

I burst into hysterics.

"It's not funny, Wyatt," Gannon snapped, then continued doing all he could to clear his throat.

"Swallowing an occasional fly is just part of the Outback experience," Roman said, trying hard not to laugh. "Happens to everyone from time to time."

As we trolled the river, I noticed bubbles rising to the

surface just off the side of our 19-foot aluminum boat. I followed the bubbles as they moved down along the side of the boat, around the 120-horsepower outboard engine and then back up the other side.

"See those bubbles?" Darla asked, pointing.

"Yes, I've been watching them," I said.

"They're from a curious croc."

"Are you joking?" Gannon asked, covering his mouth with his hands as he spoke to keep from ingesting another fly.

"Afraid not," Roman said.

"Well, couldn't it easily jump into the boat and snatch one of us?" Gannon asked.

"You bet it could," he said. "If it wanted to."

Gannon picked up his video camera and moved to a seat in the center of the boat. I did the same.

"In the heat of the day, the crocs mostly stay on the bottom of the river where it's cool," Darla explained. "They are very active at night. You can even find them two or three kilometers inland hunting for food. We never tour the river after dark, or go anywhere in the bush for that matter. It's just too dangerous."

"Right," Roman said. "At night, we could not ensure your safety."

Gannon looked at me and gulped.

Changing the subject, Darla pointed out a hibiscus tree along the shore.

"The hibiscus is a very important tree for us," she said. "It is like a store where we can get supplies and medicines."

"What do you mean?" Gannon asked, opening his journal to take notes.

"From hibiscus branches, we carve out spears. They are sturdy, flexible, and buoyant, so if we try to spear a fish and miss, it will float back to the top. And hibiscus flowers help settle an upset stomach."

"The bush right next to it," Roman said, "that's an emu bush. Also a very important plant. The leaves have antiseptic properties, so if you have a wound you can clean and wrap it with the leaves to help it heal more quickly."

Darla went on to explain how they build shelters by peeling away water resistant bark from paper trees. Paper trees can also be a source of fresh drinking water.

"See the bubbly knot on the side of the tree?" Darla asked, pointing to a tall paper tree near the shoreline.

"Yes," I said.

"That's a water catchment. Take a stick, poke a hole in the bottom, and a stream of fresh water will pour out. You can get a few liters of drinking water out of a knot that size."

"That's so cool," Gannon said.

"When you are done drinking," Roman continued, "you cork the hole with the stick so there is water left for the next person. That's the bush law."

It began to make sense how the Aboriginal people could thrive in this area. The bush provided everything a person needed to survive. Lots of food, medicines, and shelter. How they protected themselves from all the deadly creatures was another story. I was about to ask, when we saw a young kangaroo hopping along the beachhead. It came right up to the water's edge and leaned over to take a drink.

"Oh, jeez," Gannon said, pointing. "Doesn't that kangaroo know there are crocs in this river? Run kangaroo! I mean hop! Hop backward and get the heck out of here!"

"Kangaroos can't hop backwards," Darla said.

"Really? Hmmm, I didn't know that," Gannon said, then turned back to the kangaroo. "Turn around and hop forward then! Danger! Beware! Crocs everywhere!"

Gannon was right. Not far from where the kangaroo was drinking, maybe 10 to 15 feet offshore, a set of bubbles rose to the surface. I pointed them out to the others.

"I knew it!" Gannon shouted. "A croc spotted the kangaroo! Hop away! Go, go, go!"

The kangaroo, oblivious to Gannon's shouting, continued to drink from the river. We all held our breath as we watched the bubbles move closer to shore. Without a ripple, the snout and eyes of a midsized crocodile suddenly appeared above the water. Any second, that croc was going to launch at the kangaroo. I squinted my eyes, hardly able to watch. As the croc positioned itself for an ambush, the kangaroo caught sight of it and, like a dart, turned and bolted off into the forest.

"Oh—my—gosh!" Gannon said. "That was close!"

"I think that little kangaroo just learned a lesson," Darla said. "Be on guard when drinking from the river."

The croc slowly sank back into the water, making itself invisible once again.

Returning to the dockage point, we jumped ashore and moved up the hill so that we were safely away from the water's edge. After we tied the boat to a tree, Darla went ahead to set up our camp, while we caught a ride with Roman to Nourlangie to see the ancient cave paintings and the sacred cliffs known as Lightning Dreaming.

The hike took us through a section of forest that had been reduced to black sticks by a recent fire. Beyond the burn, the forest was lush and green again. High up in a tree, we saw a koala. He was chewing on leaves and far less interested in us than we were in him. Farther along, a dingo darted through a clearing and vanished silently into the forest. I also spotted the ears of two kangaroos as they hopped through the low brush, their heads appearing and disappearing with each bounce.

Nourlangie is a large rock cathedral, with high walls and elaborate cave paintings representing, among other things, Namarrgon, or "Lightning Man."

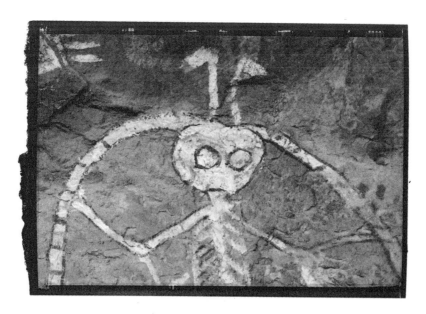
Cave painting of "Lightning Man"

Roman explained the story behind the painting.

"See the band that connects his hands and legs to his head?" he asked.

Gannon and I nodded.

"That's where Namarrgon wears his lightning. When he shoots the lightning, the bolts are his children. They are called Aljurr."

"Does Lightning Man also make the thunder?" Gannon asked.

"Good question. Yes, he makes the thunder using the stone axes on his knees."

We all studied the cave painting and I took some photos.

"Lightning Man sort of looks like a grasshopper," Gannon commented.

"Interesting you say that. His children, the lightning bolts, take the form of an orange and blue grasshopper after they hit the earth. They are called Leichardt's grasshoppers."

"After Ludwig Leichardt, the explorer?" I asked.

"That's right. Mr. Leichardt studied these grasshoppers during one of his expeditions. That's how they got the name. They return to this area at the start of each storm season, looking for their father, Namarrgon. When Aboriginal people see these grasshoppers return, they know it is time to take shelter."

"Wow, that's an amazing story!" Gannon said, as he scribbled notes in his journal.

I took some more photos of the cave paintings, then we hiked another 20 minutes or so to the Gunwarrde Warrde Lookout.

"What you see here is the home of Namarrgon," Roman said, pointing to a multilayered slab of orange rock. "It is called Lightning Dreaming."

The late afternoon sun shone on the beautiful cliffs and cast a warm tint over the long, tree-topped plateaus to the south.

"It will be dark in less than an hour," Roman said, basing his estimate on the position of the sun. "That's just enough time to hike back and drive to camp. We had better go. The wildlife will be coming out soon, and that makes driving a bit dangerous."

The cliffs called Lightning Dreaming

At the moment, we're about 30 minutes into what Roman said was an hour drive to camp. The fading light is only making Roman drive faster, despite there being more and more kangaroos off the side of the road. Fact is, this drive to camp is getting a little hairy. I better close my journal ... and hold on for dear life!

GANNON

Kangaroos are everywhere in the Northern Territory

"Roos, mate!" I shouted at the top of my lungs.

"Crikey!" Roman yelled, turning the wheel hard.

The Land Rover lurched right, wobbled and almost

tipped over. Another narrow miss. There were two of them this time, both adults. They had hopped out of the bushes onto the side of the road right in front of us. Lucky for them, Roman has quick reflexes.

It was dusk and the air had cooled, bringing the kangaroos out of the shade for an evening of hopping and frolicking, turning these lazy Outback roads into potential death traps, and that had all of us on edge. As I peered into the fading light ahead, my heart was racing.

"If we hit a kangaroo, I don't know what I'll do," I said. "It'll be awful!"

"Maybe we should slow down a little," Wyatt suggested, his voice jittery.

"Sorry, mates," Roman said. "We're racing nightfall. That's when the mimis come out."

"What's a mimi?" Wyatt asked.

"The spirits that live in the cracks of the rocks."

"Whoa, that's spooky," I said.

"Nighttime is spirit time. It's also croc time, snake time, mossie time. When the sun goes down, it's best to be in camp and to stay there."

"And mossies are . . . ?" Wyatt wondered aloud.

"Mosquitoes," I said. "You really should have brushed up on your Australian before our expedition."

Without warning, Wyatt's arm shot forward. "*ROOOOOOO!*" he screamed.

Once more, Roman swerved. The tires squealed as the

rubber strained to keep hold of the pavement. The truck rocked so violently I slid across the seat, realizing for the first time that I wasn't even buckled up. What the heck could I have been thinking? If this vehicle were to flip, I'd go crashing through the window. Immediately, I strapped myself in, pulling the seatbelt tight across my chest.

"Sorry, mates!" Roman shouted. "This is a dangerous time to drive, no way around it! Roos in Australia are like deer in the U.S.! They're everywhere and most active at night!"

"Well, now I know what the roo bars are for," I said, referring to the round metal bars that are attached to the front of the vehicle.

"Right, to protect the truck from getting smashed," Wyatt said.

"And to protect us from getting smashed, too!" Roman added. "A big roo comes through the windshield, it could kill ya!"

The thought made me shudder with fear, but Roman was pretty well spot on. Driving in the Outback at sundown was dangerous business. But as luck would have it, we made it to camp without hitting a single roo and thank goodness for that!

The very last light was fading from the sky as Roman led us on a short hike over several layers of flat stone. As we climbed higher, the breeze picked up and the air almost felt cool. A little farther up, we found Darla unrolling her sleeping pad. Nearby, she had already built a small fire pit. About

20 feet overhead, large slabs of gray rock jutted from the hill, providing some protection from the rain.

"How's this for a campsite?" she asked, tossing us each a small pillow.

"Looks like a great spot to me," I said. "Spacious, airy, and best of all, Namarrgon can't get us in here."

"That is true," Roman said with a smile.

Dinner was several strips of emu jerky, yam chips, and wild passion fruit that Roman had brought for each of us, along with some tart raspberries he picked from a bush at the trailhead.

As Wyatt and I prepared our sleeping areas, I stopped and took in our surroundings. It seemed to me this vast complex of stone was all the shelter you'd ever really need. I turned to Wyatt and posed a question:

"If you can live in a place like this, who needs a house?"

"I have to admit," Wyatt said quietly, "you have a good point."

Darla and Roman seemed tired, settling right onto their sleeping pads, covering themselves with blankets, and saying goodnight.

Because thousands of tourists visit this area each year, overnight stays are rarely permitted in these rocky caves. Typically, people are only allowed to stay in designated camping sites, which are mostly in wooded sections of the park, far from the traditional dwelling places of the Aboriginals. It was Darla and Roman's uncle, a respected elder and employee of the park service, who gave us permission to camp here at the outcropping, a place where generations of Aboriginals once lived, and we are certainly grateful.

Right now a small fire is crackling in a dirt pit to help keep away the bugs. The stars are numerous to the east. To the west, lightning flashes in the clouds. I think Darla and Roman have already fallen asleep.

"It's interesting to think of all the people who used to live here, taking what they needed from the land, educating their children, supporting one another," I said. "I can honestly feel their presence."

"Talk quietly," Wyatt whispered. "You're going to wake Darla and Roman."

I lowered my voice, but I couldn't keep totally quiet. I was too wound up.

"This place meant everything to them," I continued. "It was sacred and they treated it with respect. And other than the cave paintings, you'd never know anyone ever lived here. The land is still pristine and there's wildlife everywhere. Everything is in balance. I'm not saying we should all go back to the way it used to be, but don't you think there's something really important we can learn from the indigenous cultures? Like how they coexisted so well with the environment?"

"I do, but life is so different now. What aspects of the old ways could we apply to our life today?"

I thought for a minute.

"How about embracing their deep respect for nature," I said. "That'd be a good start, right?"

"Can't argue with that, Gannon," Wyatt said in a hushed voice, pulling the blanket up over his shoulders.

No time later, he was asleep.

In the morning, we're driving to an airstrip in Jabiru where Wyatt and I will catch a bush plane to a koala preserve deep in the Outback. The following day, we'll meet Darla and Roman at a research outpost and go look for some prehistoric animal fossils. We're talking Aussie dinosaur bones, baby!

Okay, that's about enough writing for one night. The fire is dying out and it's time to catch some zzz's.

G'night, Darla, Roman, and Wyatt.

G'night mimis.

G'night Namarrgon.

WYATT

MARCH 14, 9:02 AM
JABIRU, NORTHERN TERRITORY
81° FAHRENHEIT, 27° CELSIUS

Early this morning, we gathered up our gear, hiked down from the rock outcropping and drove to the Jabiru airport, a single strip of asphalt just long enough for small planes to take off and land.

Cessna Caravan, Jabiru airport, pre-flight

We were greeted by "Bush Pilot Pete" and took a seat at a picnic table outside the hangar where he'd set out a simple breakfast. Over oatmeal, fruit, toast, and tea, we got to know each other a little bit. Pete's a friendly, humorous guy in his mid-30s. His father was a naturalist from Scotland who fell in love with the Outback. During one of his expeditions he met a woman, married her, and never left. So Pete's half Scottish, half Aboriginal or, as he put it, "A beautiful mix of cultures!" He's been a bush pilot for the past fifteen years, has a stellar reputation, and is a dear friend of Roman and Darla. I do not think we could have found a more qualified pilot if we'd tried.

As I write, Pete is finishing up his pre-flight inspection. The plane is a Cessna Caravan and seats eight. Since we only have three, there will be plenty of room for our packs and equipment. With departure nearing, Gannon and I should probably do another gear check ourselves. My brother says I'm obsessive about it, always checking and checking again, but before embarking on an expedition I want to be absolutely sure we have everything we need. I also want to say goodbye to Darla and Roman and let them know how excited we are to rejoin them in a couple days for the fossil expedition.

I see Pete jogging back this way. That means it's about time for lift off. I'll report again from our next camp.

GANNON

MARCH 14
FLIGHT FROM DARWIN TO THE KOALA PRESERVE

I was just dozing off when our bush plane was rocked by an explosion!

The sound was deafening, like someone had shot off a cannon right next to my ear. A ringing sound filled the inside of my head. The plane dropped and my stomach lifted into my throat. I took hold of the pilot's seat in front of me. When the plane caught, I felt like I'd been punched in the gut.

Our bush pilot, Pete, grabbed the headphones from around his neck and put them over his ears.

"Mayday! Mayday!" Pete shouted into the microphone. "Victor-Henry-Sally-Liam-Mary! We're in big trouble up here!" He flipped a few switches on the radio and paused to listen. After a moment, he ripped the headphones from his ears and tossed them to the ground. "The explosion knocked out the radio!"

"At least the propeller is still working!" Wyatt shouted.

"Yeah, thank goodness for that!" I yelled.

The words had hardly passed my lips when flames rose up in the cockpit like some kind of demonic orange ghost. Pete started to squirm, frantically stomping at the fire with his boots. Wyatt grabbed the fire extinguisher from between the seats and shot a burst of foam onto it, quickly extinguishing the blaze and filling the plane with a swirling white mist.

"That was quick thinking!" Pete shouted, and began to cough. "Good on ya, mate!"

We were all choking on the dense smoke that was circulating through the cockpit. I pulled my shirt up over my mouth and nose and Pete opened the vents. A loud whooshing sound came into the plane and just like that, the air cleared.

Despite the damage, the plane hummed along steadily. Fresh air circulated throughout the cabin. I inhaled deeply, trying to settle my nerves. As I looked down to tighten my seatbelt, something else in the engine blew—a second explosion, this one even louder than the first! I looked up just in time to see a ball of flames shoot up and over the cockpit. Oil splattered across the windshield. Black smoke poured from the engine, making it even more difficult to see.

"Agh, bugger!" I heard Pete yell, along with some other choice words my mom wouldn't care to read in my journal.

The dark smoke cleared just in time for me to watch the mangled propeller sputter and stall. Just like that, the roaring hum of the engine went quiet. The only sound now was the wind whistling through a small section of the plane's shell that had been ripped open by the explosion.

Our single engine Cessna Caravan was en route to a koala preserve a couple hours south of Jabiru, and from what I could see out the window, we were nowhere near civilization.

"Any chance we can make it to the nearest runway?" I asked, more or less knowing the answer.

"Not without a propeller!" Pete yelled back. "There aren't any runways out here!"

"So what's the plan?" I asked.

"No plan, mate! We're going down! It's just a matter of where!"

Below us was vast, rugged terrain—granite plateaus and rocky cliffs, jungles, swamps, and rivers—serious wilderness from one horizon to the next. Desolate and deadly country.

Arnhem Land's dramatic landscape includes Jim Jim Falls

I leaned forward to check the dashboard dials.

Altimeter: 4,900 feet and falling fast.

Speedometer: 147 knots.

I yelled to Wyatt: "How many miles per hour is one hundred and forty-seven knots?"

"One knot equals one point one five miles per hour,"

Wyatt said, "so that's about one hundred and seventy miles per hour!"

Impressive, I thought. Even in the midst of an emergency, my nerdy brother's brain works like a computer. What his computation told me was that we were flying at the speed of a Formula One race car.

"Hitting the ground at that speed probably won't go so well!" I shouted.

"Oh, you think?" Wyatt yelled back.

Due to the heat outside and the warped condition of the plane, we were being jostled all over the place, bouncing up and down, up and down. An emptiness spread through my stomach and into my chest. I wanted to scream, to let my fear be heard. No, don't do it, I told myself. You've had a good life. You've been brave. Well, not always, but mostly. Don't go out screaming like a baby. Seriously, Gannon! Do not be *that* guy!

As it turns out, I was not that guy.

Wyatt was.

"I don't want to die!" he screamed at the top of his lungs.

"That makes two of us, mate!" Pete shouted.

"Make that three!" I yelled.

Pete kept a tight grip on the throttle, moving it this way and that while trying his best to see through the smoke and oil-splattered windshield. Regardless of how futile his efforts may have been, I appreciated it. He was doing all he could.

That's when an idea hit me.

"Hey!" I shouted. "Why don't we use the parachutes?"

"Great thinking, Gannon!" Wyatt yelled, his eyes suddenly sparkling. "I'll get them! Where are they, Pete?"

"Sorry, mates!" Pete yelled. "There aren't any!"

"What!" Wyatt cried out. "Why not?"

"These planes are designed to glide if the engine fails!"

"But what if the engine blows up and tears a hole in the plane?"

"Almost never happens! That's why we don't pack chutes! But I'm thinking that policy might need to be revised!"

"Might? Uh-uh. It *definitely* needs to be revised!"

"So what are we supposed to do?" Wyatt asked.

"Only one option, mates!"

"And that is?" I asked.

"Prepare to crash!"

This is the end, I thought. Our plane is going down and there isn't a thing I can do about it. Coming to this realization, something really strange happened. Something I would not have expected in a million years. Almost like magic, my fear vanished. I mean, if someone had asked me how I thought I might react if I were ever on a plane that was about to crash, I'd have bet my life's savings that I'd be sobbing like a baby all the way to the ground. But that's not what happened. By some miracle, I actually felt calm.

The unique beauty of the Australian Outback also had a soothing effect on me. I know this might sound weird, but on occasion I have wondered how I will die. Not only how, but where. I'm not saying I dwell on it or anything. It's just a fleeting thought I have from time to time, which probably isn't all that unusual for explorers. I mean, let's face it, we put ourselves in dangerous situations on a fairly regular basis. And when you do that, it's hard *not* to think about death. Anyway, knowing that this spectacular, awe-inspiring expanse of nature would likely be my final resting place was oddly and inexplicably okay with me. And just think of the headlines:

EXPLORERS GANNON AND WYATT AND
"BUSH PILOT" PETE
CRASH IN THE AUSTRALIAN OUTBACK.
PRESUMED DEAD!

Totally intriguing, right? I mean, if it's your time to go, you may as well get some good press out of it.

As we dropped in altitude, I watched the shadow of the plane race across the rocks and through the trees. The feeling that came over me at this point was one of sadness more than anything. Sadness and regret. The regrets weren't about all the things I'd hoped to accomplish in my life, like becoming a professional filmmaker or traveling to places I'd never been or writing an epic, 1,000 page adventure novel. It had to do with my family. I was sad that I wouldn't be able to spend more time with them, that we'd never again have the chance to laugh together or hug one another. Basically, I was sad that we wouldn't be able to grow old as a family. I began thinking about the simple moments I'd often over-looked—like hanging out in our cabin, playing cards, reading books by the fire, or watching a movie together on the couch, just quietly enjoying one another's company. What I realized as the plane came nearer and nearer to the ground, is that those seemingly insignificant moments in life, they mean everything!

Suddenly, the plane tilted, hit an air pocket and dropped sharply. I looked at my brother. He had a death grip on his armrests and the color had pretty much gone out of his face.

"Hey, Wyatt!" I shouted. "You know that one time I really got on your nerves?"

"One time?" he yelled back. "I could name a thousand times that you got on my nerves!"

"Okay, fine! *Those* times! I just want to say, I'm really sorry!"

The plane lurched, hit another air pocket and dropped even closer to the ground. Wyatt turned and looked at me, his eyes were as round as golf balls.

"I'm sorry, too!" Wyatt shouted. "I'm sorry for anything and everything I've ever done that got on your nerves! Fact is, you're the best brother anyone could ever hope for. I really mean that!"

I almost teared up.

"I feel the same way about you, Wyatt!"

We both leaned into the aisle and hugged it out, manly style, with a few swift slaps to the back.

The plane shuddered violently, causing Wyatt and I to snap back into our seats. Pete made some adjustments, but I don't know that they did any good. We were falling fast.

"Sorry it had go down like this, mates!" Pete yelled. "Plenty of pilots have crashed in the bush! I just never thought it would happen to me!"

"We sure are glad we could be with you when it did!" I hollered.

That got a good laugh out of Pete.

"I was hoping we'd find a clearing, but there are too many trees! All right, mates! Assume the crash position!"

"Wait, what is the crash position?" Wyatt asked.

"Are you serious?" I shouted in disbelief. "Our mom is a flight attendant and you don't know the crash position? She would be so disappointed!"

"Just put your head between your legs!" Pete shouted.

"And kiss your butt goodbye, right?" I added.

Again, Pete laughed.

Wyatt did, too.

It seemed appropriate that my very last words would be a joke.

"Altitude, one hundred meters!" Pete shouted.

I looked out the window. We were just high enough to see the far horizon. The sun, big and bright, was still on the ascent. Below the sun were white wispy clouds so thin they cast no shadows on the landscape. Further east, some impressive thunder boomers were developing.

"Altitude fifty meters!" Pete yelled. "God bless, mates!"

I took one last look at Pete, who was pulling back on the throttle and pushing on the right rudder pedal, doing his best to bring us down smoothly in some kind of clearing. What seemed more likely is that the plane, and those in it, would be torn to pieces upon impact.

Leaning forward, I took a deep breath, put my head between my knees and closed my eyes. The plane continued to be jostled as we fell. The anticipation was agonizing. I just hoped I'd be knocked unconscious and that the end would come quickly.

And then it happened . . .

We hit the ground with a thunderous crash!

The plane tore through the trees and shrubs, snapping the left wing clear off. The sound of it all was unnatural, sickening, the type of sound no one should ever have to hear. Windows shattered and tore away. Dust filled the cabin. I couldn't see much through the swirling haze, but felt every movement. The plane toppled sideways and began flipping over, I don't know how many times, before finally coming to rest upside down. My sight was blurred by dizziness. My head throbbed. I felt like I might be sick.

Then there was silence.

"All those alive, say your name," Pete said, his words sounding slurred.

"Wyatt."

"Um, Gannon, I think."

"Thank heavens," Pete said.

When he put his hand to his head, he began to moan.

"Hey, you okay, Pete?" I asked.

"Smashed my head pretty good, but I think I'll live."

All of a sudden, a strong odor filled the inside of the plane.

"That's petrol," Pete said, his tone now urgent. "Grab what you can and get out before this bird bursts into flames!"

As fast as we could, we unbelted ourselves and dropped head first onto the plane's crushed ceiling. Still disoriented, I looked around for my backpack, but couldn't find it anywhere.

"Wyatt, do you see my backpack?"

"No, I don't."

Pete managed to push the door open and crawl outside.

"Forget the pack," he said. "Just get out!"

Wyatt went next, crawling quickly though the wreckage and out the pilot door. I tried to turn around and follow him, but the bottom flap of my shirt snagged tight on something and wouldn't come loose. I was stuck!

"I need a knife or something!" I yelled in a panic. "Quick, anything to cut my shirt! I'm stuck!"

Smoke began to fill the plane.

"Hurry, mate!" Pete shouted. "You're running out of time!"

"Here, catch this," Wyatt said, and tossed his pocketknife inside.

I caught it, opened the blade and began frantically cutting my shirt where it was caught.

"There's fire under the dash!" Wyatt yelled. "You've got to get out of there, Gannon! I mean it! Now!"

"I'm trying, trust me!" I said.

I jammed the knife through the shirt, ripping open a wide hole. With a hard tug, the shirt finally tore away. I was free!

Wyatt had crawled back inside and was pulling me through the door. Once outside the plane, we stood up and ran a short distance away, taking cover behind a cluster of trees.

"Would you believe it?" Wyatt said, ecstatically. "Not a single broken bone."

Before I could respond, there was a hiss, crackle, and a magnificent *KA-BOOM*!

The force of the explosion knocked us all to the ground. Shards of metal went whizzing by like bullets, tearing through the leaves. Flaming pieces of the plane tumbled over the rocks and landed nearby.

"Stay down and cover your head!" Wyatt shouted, still on the ground.

Metal rained down all around us. A small piece landed on my thigh, burned right through my shorts and singed my skin. I could hear it sizzling and quickly rolled over to flick it off. When I did, the hot metal fell into the sand, leaving a raw, red triangular shape where it had burned my skin clean off.

"Is everyone okay?" Wyatt asked. "No one was hit by any shrapnel, I hope?"

"No shrapnel here." Pete said. "How about you Gannon?"

"I got burned by a piece, but I'll be fine."

"Pete, your head," Wyatt said, pointing to his own.

Pete gently touched his head, winced and looked at his hand. His palm was covered in bright red blood. Wyatt and I walked over and knelt by his side.

"I knew I took a good whack on the melon when the plane tumbled," he said. "Must have sliced it open, too. Didn't even notice the blood. But now that you've pointed it out, mates, I'm feeling a bit woozy."

"Move into the shade and lie down," Wyatt said. "I'll take a closer look."

Pete crawled under a tree and Wyatt examined his wound. On the left side of his forehead was a deep gash. Three, maybe four inches long. There was no question, Pete needed stitches.

"I have to be honest," Wyatt said. "It's pretty serious. Rest up while Gannon and I look around for the first aid kit."

Whatever was still inside the plane had obviously been destroyed by the explosion, but some of our gear had been ejected when we hit the ground. Looking at the wreckage, it appeared that the plane had skidded and rolled several hundred feet before coming to rest. Wyatt and I searched the entire area to see what we could recover. My brother made the good point that every salvageable item could be key to our survival, so we were extremely careful in our search.

Swatting at flies and wary of snakes, we scanned far and

wide to be sure we wouldn't miss anything. By the time we'd finished, we had found Pete's gun case and rifle, two of the six canteens, one small container of sandwiches, some scattered remnants of the first aid kit, Wyatt's backpack, a box of waterproof matches, a headlamp, and my journal, which had been tossed from the seat pocket when we crashed. We also gathered up a few slightly charred but still usable seat cushions and woolen blankets. Wyatt took his camera from his backpack, found that it still worked, and put it away to save the battery. My backpack, video camera, the whistles and radio, and both of our Akubras were lost in the fire. Oh, yeah . . . and most of our food.

Stopping to stare at the plane, I fell into a trance. The last of the orange flames were quietly flickering, the paint on the fuselage was bubbling and melting away, everything was turning black. A few nearby trees and shrubs had been scorched pretty good, too, but the blaze had not spread. When the fire finally died all that was left were the plane's mangled remains. It looked like the stripped away carcass of a giant crow. All three of us could have been lying amongst that charred wreckage. Dead. With that thought came a wave of emotion that was too much to handle. I hid myself behind a tree, fell to my knees and sobbed uncontrollably.

Gathering myself, I walked back to where Pete was resting. Along the way, my brain shifted gears, moving from relief to dread. Yes, we survived. And, for the most part, we are all okay. That's great and all, but we can't kid ourselves. We're far from safe. I mean, first off, how will anyone ever find us out here? I honestly don't know that a rescue plane will be able to spot the crash under this high canopy of trees. Besides that, how many deadly predators and snakes are there within a one-mile radius of where I stand? How many days, or even hours, before we're confronted by a huge croc, a poisonous snake, or a hungry pack of dingoes? What if the cut on Pete's head gets infected? And most of our food was destroyed. All that's left is a meal's worth for each of us, two small meals each at best.

Jeez, there's so much to consider. We need to huddle up, put our heads together, and make a plan. I mean, without a plan, and I'm talking a smart one, we may never be heard from again!

WYATT

MARCH 14, 4:41 PM
OUTBACK, NORTHERN TERRITORY
95° FAHRENHEIT, 35° CELSIUS
WIND: 0-5 MPH

Pete is in bad shape. He seems to be getting worse with each passing hour. It's not so much the wound, which we closed up the best we could with butterfly stitches that we found amongst the debris, as it is the blow he took to his head. He's been complaining of dizziness, is unable to walk without staggering, and has felt nauseous from time to time. He's also confused, and isn't making a whole lot of sense. These are all symptoms of a major concussion and that worries me.

"So, what's our plan, Wyatt?" Gannon asked, pacing back and forth.

I shrugged my shoulders.

"I knew it," he said, talking a mile a minute. "We don't have a plan, but we definitely need a plan because without a plan we're going to die!"

Pete rolled over slowly to face us.

"Seeing as we're in Woop Woop," he said so quietly I had to move closer to him to hear, "I think our best bet is to hang tight and await rescue."

"Woop Woop? What the heck is Woop Woop?" Gannon asked.

"It's just an expression, mate. Means we're in the middle of nowhere."

"But there's all kinds of things out here that can kill us," Gannon continued. "Isn't it only a matter of time before something sniffs us out?"

"If we try to hike to safety, our chances of running into predators would be even greater," I said. "We don't have maps or a GPS or anything that can help us navigate. Basically, we'd just be wandering around in the Outback, and that could get us into even more trouble."

"What if we climb to the top of one of those rocky plateaus we flew over?" Gannon suggested. "Maybe from up there we would see something, or maybe someone would see us."

"We'll consider that later," I said, "but for now I agree with Pete. Let's stay here, near the wreckage, and keep our fingers crossed that someone spots it. At some point, Darla and Roman will get word that we didn't arrive and will send out a search party."

What worries me most is our location. We are in an extremely remote area. I hadn't seen a town, not even a road, since we took off from the airport and we were flying for more than an hour.

"Another thing I should probably mention," Pete said, his voice still weak.

"What's that?" Gannon asked.

"I'm afraid we may have gone down on forbidden Aboriginal lands."

"Forbidden?" Gannon asked. "What do you mean forbidden?"

"We were flying near the border of Arnhem Land and I realized that I'd drifted slightly off course. Before I could correct the flight path, the engine blew."

"But why is Arnhem Land forbidden?"

"The government turned this land back over to the traditional owners. Anyone else needs approval before entering. Even me, since I was born in another part of Australia. And, well, I don't have it. I've heard it's not a place you want to be found trespassing."

"Why? What could happen?"

"The locals are very protective of their land and apparently some of them don't take kindly to strangers."

"Well, isn't that great," Gannon said, throwing up his arms. "Not only did we crash, but we're trespassing, too."

"Forget about it, Gannon," I said. "We only have to worry about that if the wildlife doesn't get us first."

"And that's supposed to make me feel better *how?*"

Pete let his head fall back in the dirt and began to groan.

"You going to be okay, Pete?" I asked.

"I don't know, mates. My head is killing me. My ears won't stop ringing either."

Pete looked pale.

"Here, use this as a pillow," I said, taking one of the seat cushions we'd salvaged and placing it under his head.

"Thanks, Wyatt. Maybe I'll improve if I get a little rest."

Pete slid his hat over his eyes.

"Gannon, you want to take first watch?" I asked. "I could use an hour or so of rest, if you're okay with it."

"Yeah, I guess," Gannon said, still pacing.

"Thanks."

"Wait, remind me. What am I keeping an eye out for?"

"Rescue planes or anything that could kill us."

"And if something that could kill us happens to pay a visit, I do what exactly? Ask them to please go away?"

"Just wake me. Worst case scenario, we have Pete's rifle."

"Jeez," Gannon said, running his hand through his hair. "I hope it doesn't come to that." Pete rolled over. His eyes were glassy, and at half-mast.

"It may come to that," he said. "Keep on the lookout for dingoes especially."

"Okay," Gannon said, his voice cracking.

"Dingoes can be unpredictable, but they're usually skittish around humans. If any get too close, just fire a warning shot into the air and they should scatter. But if it comes down to you or the dingo, don't think twice. Just shoot it."

The idea that we might have to shoot an animal is not ideal. But, it's like Pete said, if we're attacked, what choice do we have?

There's this thing out here Australians call "Bushcraft." It basically means having the skills necessary to survive in the bush. Fact is, Gannon and I would rank quite low on the Bushcraft scale. That's not to say we don't have outdoor survival experience. We do, but the environment here is new to us. What we do know, which is little, comes from the reading assignments my mom gave us and yesterday's tour of Kakadu with Darla and Roman. As much as I do not want to admit it, I think Pete's rifle is going to be critical to our survival.

GANNON

LATE AFTERNOON

When I checked on Pete, there were flies crawling all over his wound. He was asleep, so I waved them away, but they came right back. The first aid kit was torn apart in the crash and aside from the butterfly tape, we didn't find much else that was useful. No alcohol wipes or antiseptic ointments. With all these dirty flies buzzing around, I felt like we needed to do something to keep his cut from becoming infected. Aside from that, my burn needed cleaning, too.

Flipping through my journal I read some of the notes I had taken during our river tour with Darla and Roman. They had told us how certain trees and shrubs can cure all kinds of ailments and that gave me an idea. Maybe there was a plant nearby that we could use to treat our wounds!

I woke Wyatt and ran the idea by him.

"Good thinking, Gannon," my brother said, paying me a rare compliment. "I remember them saying something about a plant they used for cuts. What was it?"

Returning to my journal, I found where I'd written "Bush Medicines" and underneath, "Hibiscus" and "Emu Bush," with some notes next to each. I read it aloud to Wyatt.

"The leaves of an Emu Bush can be used to clean wounds. They have an antiseptic property that helps fight off infection. The hibiscus flower, when eaten, will settle your stomach if you feel nauseous."

I set my journal down and looked at Wyatt.

"Roman and Darla pointed both of them out to us," I said. "Do you remember what they look like?"

"I do," Wyatt said and looked around. "Pete's actually sleeping under a hibiscus. And, look, there's an emu bush at the bottom of the hill. The one with the small pink flowers."

Wyatt and I ran to the emu bush and each picked a

handful of leaves. We then hiked back up the hill and pulled several fully bloomed hibiscus flowers off the tree. Our hands full, we took our bounty to where Pete was sleeping.

"Should we wake him?" I asked.

"We need to," Wyatt said. "The longer we wait, the more likely it is that he'll get an infection."

We woke Pete. He was groggy and disoriented. Wyatt told him to stay put, that we were just going to place a few leaves over his cut to speed up the healing process.

"Also, if you have it in you to eat this flower," I said, "it might help your stomach."

"Thanks, mates," Pete said quietly. "Quite thoughtful of you."

Once we had tended to Pete, he went back to sleep almost immediately. I took some time to carefully clean my burn, then helped Wyatt gather fallen branches to build a shelter.

Positioning the branches in an upside down "V" shape, we secured them together with a natural rope we'd made by peeling the outer layer of bark from the hibiscus and weaving it through the branches, another trick Darla had taught us. After the frame was built, we tore away strips of bark from a nearby paper tree and laid them over the top of the frame, again securing the strips with hibiscus rope. The paper bark is waterproof and will keep us dry if it rains.

I went looking for one last sturdy branch to help support the shelter. Eventually I spotted one lying atop a pile of leaves at the base of a gully, but when I leaned over and lifted the branch, I nearly jumped out of my boots! Coiled underneath was an eastern brown snake! The second most venomous snake in the world!

The eastern brown took off like a shot, slithering right between my feet! I quickly spread my legs wide and jumped forward, trying to put myself out of striking distance. The snake kept its pace, moving rapidly down the hill and I soon lost sight of it, probably because I turned and ran in the other direction.

Still panting, I told Wyatt.

"You're sure it was an eastern brown?" Wyatt asked.

"Sure I'm sure," I said. "I saw it clear as day."

Wyatt walked slowly down the hill in the direction it had slithered, and found it partially coiled near a fallen log.

"Yep, it's an eastern brown all right," he said.

"I told you! We can't just leave it there, can we? It might come back up the hill and bite us all!"

"Maybe we should shoot it."

"Is that really the best option?" I asked. "I mean, I don't like the idea of shooting anything."

"I don't either. But if we're bitten by this thing, we die. It's that simple."

"I also think we need to save the bullets just in case we have to use them against something larger."

"That's a good point. Then we'll have to chase it off somehow. If we can scare it away, I doubt it will come back."

"Be my guest," I said, handing Wyatt the branch I'd just grabbed, which was probably four feet in length.

"Thanks," he said, sarcastically.

The snake was in no mood to be bothered. After Wyatt swatted at it a few times with the branch, it decided to relocate. We followed it, chasing after the thing and yelling and stomping and swinging the stick until it was a good distance from camp. Finally, it disappeared into the dense underbrush.

"I think that snake got the message," Wyatt said. "I doubt it will risk coming back this way."

Boy, I sure hope he's right!

GANNON

MARCH 15, EARLY MORNING

Wow, almost hard to believe, but we seemed to have made it though the first night without incident. Okay, truth be told, Wyatt woke me around 3 a.m. and told me to stay on watch until 6, and well, how should I put this? Let's just say I might have drifted off to sleep for a stretch. But, hey, here we are, safe and sound at sunrise! No harm no foul, right?

Ooof, stomach's a rumblin'! Yeah, think it's about time to dig into that food we salvaged.

WYATT

"Okay, fine," Gannon said, pausing to swallow hard, "maybe the Vegemite sandwiches weren't such a great idea."

"Being stranded in the Outback with nothing else to eat, you'd think that just about anything would taste good," I said, "but I'm having a tough time forcing this down."

Pete, still lying on his back, said. "It's an acquired taste, I suppose," his words slow and drawn out. "Did you pack anything else to eat?"

"Loads of stuff," Gannon said, "but it all got destroyed in the crash. Unfortunately the only container that survived was the one I used to pack up all the Vegemite sandwiches."

Vegemite is a dark brown spread that basically tastes like some kind of salty, meat paste. If that sounds disgusting, then I've described it well.

"I assume you didn't actually taste the Vegemite before you decided to make all these sandwiches," I said.

"Had no reason to. I thought it'd be delicious. The clerk at the store said Vegemite is like Australia's peanut butter."

"The clerk probably meant that Australians eat it on bread all the time," I said, "the same way Americans eat peanut butter."

"Ahhh," Gannon said. "That must have been what he meant. Hey, at least these sandwiches will keep us fed through tonight. We can't complain about that."

True, but I'm already dreaming about the spicy curry noodle bowl I'll have as soon as we make it back to civilization. For now, looks like my only choice is to overcome my gag reflexes and force the rest of this sandwich down the hatch.

GANNON

MIDDAY

So, this is bad! I'm talking, *as-bad-as-it-gets* bad!

See, Wyatt was exhausted and had been dragging all morning so I told him to go take a nap, that I'd stand guard, right? Well, while he was resting, I totally dozed off *(AGAIN!)* and when I woke, Pete was gone! He must have wandered off or something. Obviously, this is all my fault and I feel just terrible about it.

I don't get it, though. I mean, why would Pete just up and leave camp? After all, he's the one who said we should stay put and wait for someone to find us.

Then *poof*, he up and vanishes!

Wyatt thinks he must have woken up a little loopy from his head injury and wandered off without really knowing what he was doing. It doesn't look like he took anything either. He even left his canteen and rifle. Initially, that made me think he'd be right back, but it's been a couple hours and still no sign of Pete!

Oh, man, trekking through the bush all alone, and in his state of mind, no less, it's a death sentence! Seriously, if we don't find him, I don't know that he'll make it through the night!

WYATT

MARCH 15, 11:33 PM
OUTBACK, AUSTRALIA
81° FAHRENHEIT, 27° CELSIUS
WIND: 0-10 MPH

Despite an aggressive search that lasted most of the afternoon, we found no trace of Pete. Worse, we wandered too far away from the camp we'd made at the wreckage and cannot find our way back. We took Pete's rifle, the canteens and my backpack. Everything else was left behind under the assumption we'd be back. I'm so upset with Gannon for falling asleep during his watch, but blame myself for not being more careful about marking our path from camp.

We have now been marooned in the Outback for 36 hours. The fact that we didn't see or hear a single rescue plane all day is concerning. Is it possible that Pete was further off course than he thought? The air traffic controller in Jabiru knew we were en route to the koala preserve, and so did Darla and Roman. The director of the facility was expecting us, too, so we have to assume that a search is underway. Maybe by now our parents are even en route to join the effort.

Gannon and I have set up a small shelter atop some flat rocks and I have Pete's rifle by my side with the safety on. We're in a relatively safe spot, I think, high off the swampy floor, but every time I hear something, I pick up the rifle, point the barrel into the darkness, click off the safety and put my finger on the trigger. So far, I have not had to use it.

Earlier, Gannon found some fresh water, a bubble in a paper tree, like Darla showed us. I poked a small hole in the bubble and filled our canteens, then re-corked it, as Gannon reminded me that it's "Bush Law" to do so. We are hydrated and have a decent amount of water left, but we are completely out of food and terribly hungry.

Our only chances now are 1) Pete miraculously making it to safety and sending out help or 2) a plane flying overhead tomorrow and spotting us.

In the morning, we'll continue our search for Pete, trekking in what we feel is the easiest and most logical path to travel by foot. In other words, the path of least resistance. Pete needs our help, and I believe this plan will give us the best chance of finding him. It will also increase our chances of reaching safety.

I better get some sleep.

Our search resumes at dawn.

GANNON

MARCH 16
LUNCH TIME, ONLY I DON'T HAVE ANY LUNCH

After a second night in the bush, this one more restless than the last, we're totally spent and lost and desperate and if I'm being totally honest, a little confused about what to do next. Okay, a lot confused.

Last night at some pitch-black hour I was startled by the sound of dingoes moving around below the rocks where we'd set up camp. Just knowing they were down there kept me up worrying the better part of the night. I know Wyatt had the rifle handy and all, but come on, it's not like he's some kind of expert marksman or anything! Actually, other than a paint ball battle we had with our cousins last year, I don't think he's ever fired a gun in his life.

Here's the thing: those dingoes are no dummies. They know we're here and that we'd make for a decent meal. Come to think of it, I wouldn't be surprised if they're silently stalking us right now, just waiting for the right time to attack.

All day we've been yelling Pete's name as loud as we can. We hope he'll eventually hear us and yell back and that we'll find him safe, but so far we haven't heard a peep.

Breaking our spirits into even smaller pieces is this vile heat. I'm not exaggerating, before the sun even comes over the horizon the air is already soupy with humidity. It's early afternoon now and even hotter, which I didn't think possible.

There are big, puffy white clouds forming to the north that I'm praying will give us some relief from the sun. I'd even welcome some rain right now, just to cool things down, allow us to collect some more fresh drinking water, and keep the crazy flies away for a while. There are so many of those little winged nuisances buzzing around my face right now, I can hardly stand it. I have to continuously exhale through my nose in quick bursts just to keep them from crawling up my nostrils. And if I don't keep my eyes squinted, they'll literally land right on my eyeball.

The only thing that brings me any relief at all is watching Wyatt swing wildly at them, trying to defend himself from their relentless pestering. We've got nothing to laugh at, but I can't help myself. I mean, it's pretty darn funny. Just a few minutes ago he actually snapped, got up and ran in circles, swinging his arms around like a madman.

"These flies! I can't take it anymore!" he shouted.

"We have to get used to them, mate," I said. "They aren't going anywhere!"

"First off, don't call me mate!" Wyatt yelled, smacking himself repeatedly in the face. "Second, it's impossible to get used to them! That's why I bought a fly net! Ugh, I could kill you for stealing it!"

Oh, yeah, and there's that. After being so bothered by the flies on the East Alligator River, I secretly slipped his fly net out of his camera case and put it in my backpack, thinking it would be funny to see him frantically looking for it the next time the flies swarmed, only to glance over at me and find it draped over my smiling face. Unfortunately, my backpack and everything in it was turned to ash in the crash, so, yeah, no more net.

Anyhow, Wyatt eventually wore himself out doing that awkward fly swatting dance or whatever it was. Seriously, if I had the time, I'd make a cave painting of his wacky performance and called it, "Lunatic Man."

Right now he's resting in the shade, totally whipped, a shirt wrapped around his face like a mummy. You know, that's actually not a bad idea. Think I'm going to wrap myself up, too.

Okay, mummification time.

Gannon out!

WYATT

MARCH 17, 3:19 AM
OUTBACK, AUSTRALIA
80° FAHRENHEIT, 27° CELSIUS
WIND: CALM

It's my shift to keep watch while Gannon sleeps. I am stoking a fire I got started with the waterproof matches and have the rifle at my side. In the distance, I hear the occasional rumble of thunder, though the rain has held off. There aren't many flies around at the moment, but every other creature in the Outback comes alive once night falls. All around our camp, I hear noises. I am trying not to worry, but that's a challenge.

To occupy my mind and pass the time until morning, I've been reading by headlamp the journals of the ill-fated Burke and Wills Expedition, which I brought in my backpack. In 1860—1861, Robert O'Hara Burke and William John Wills were attempting to cross Australia from Melbourne in the south to the Gulf of Carpentaria in the north, a journey of more than 2,000 miles. At the time, most of the Australian interior had not been explored by non-indigenous people. Therefore, their mission was to document and map the interior, record the weather, and sketch much of what they saw along the way—a lot like what Gannon and I do on our expeditions, only we take photos and video now, instead of making sketches.

Many historians say the mission was doomed from the start, due to Burke's inexperience as an explorer. He had never been on an expedition, much less led one. His knowledge of the bush was limited, and he had little in the way of wilderness survival skills. What's more, Burke was unorganized, disliked hot weather, and had a fiery temper. I was wondering why someone like that would be appointed expedition leader, when I read that he had good friends within the ranks of the Royal Society of Victoria, the organization that funded the expedition.

The expedition left from Melbourne's Royal Park on August 20, 1860. There was so much excitement over their journey, nearly 15,000 people turned up to see them off. Despite Burke's failings as a leader, the expedition team made it all the way to the north coast, most likely a credit to the leadership of Wills, who was second in command. It was on the return trip to the south that disaster struck. Seven men died en route to Melbourne, including Burke and Wills.

Below is an excerpt from one of William John Wills' last journal entries, dated June 26, 1861:

> Clear cold night, slight breeze from the E., day beautifully warm and pleasant. Mr. Burke suffers greatly from the cold, and is getting extremely weak. I am weaker than ever although I have a good appetite, and relish the nardoo much, but it seems to give us no nutriment, and the birds here are so shy as not to be got at. Even if we got a good supply of fish, I doubt whether we could do much work on them and the nardoo alone. Nothing now but the greatest good luck can save any of us; and as for myself, I may live four or five days if the weather continues warm. My pulse are at forty-eight, and very weak, and my legs and arms are nearly skin and bone.

Nardoo is a plant that looks just like a clover, so it is easy to see why that would not keep them alive very long. At this point, Burke no longer had the strength to walk, so Wills and a few others went on one "last look" for food. Wills never made it back, dying in the desert of starvation.

Historians believe that if Burke and Wills had stayed closer to the friendly Aboriginals who fed them when they were in need, they would have survived. But Burke apparently insulted them, refusing their food. Little did he know, the Aboriginals had thrived in this harsh landscape for tens of thousands of years. I suppose he learned his lesson the hard way. When members of the expedition returned to Burke, they found that he had also died of starvation.

For obvious reasons, this is not a reassuring story.

I just tossed some more wood in the pit and brought the fire back. Since I still have some time before my watch ends, I will make note of an idea that just came to mind. To keep the flies off of us, we have been wrapping our faces with t-shirts. Since the shirts are cotton, they don't allow for much ventilation and are uncomfortable as a result. What I just remembered is that inside my backpack are two large mesh pockets. So I am going to cut them out with my pocketknife and see if I can stitch together a pair of breathable fly nets.

Time to get to work.

GANNON

AFTERNOON

Status Update: We've been stranded out here for a few days now and if we're out here much longer this could very well be my brother's final resting place . . . because I am about to pummel him into the ground!

I mean, jeez, is he getting on my nerves! Okay, fine, I'm

probably getting on his, too, but he's more to blame than me. And that's an unbiased fact. Honest!

Sure, he did make us some awesome fly nets out of the mesh lining in his pack last night, and I'll admit, those nets have been a total game changer. It's just that overall his attitude today is about as sour as a bag of lemons.

After a few hours of hiking this morning, with no sign of Pete anywhere, we stopped for a rest.

"My body and mind are shutting down," Wyatt said. "We're never going to find Pete, and if I don't eat soon, I don't know how much longer I can keep hiking. I'm telling you, Gannon, we're going out just like Burke and Wills. Or, worse, we'll die and no one will ever find us, just like Ludwig Leichardt."

He was lying on his back in the leaves, his arms fanned out to the side, like he was about to make a "leaf angel."

"Come on, Mr. Positive," I said. "This isn't like you at all."

I walked over to Wyatt and lifted him under the arms.

"Get off me," he said, and shook free.

"I'm just trying to get you over to the shade. The sun will turn you into a piece of beef jerky before the day's out."

To tell the truth, by this time Wyatt already looked like a cooked steak. His face was beet red, cracked and peeling in places. His lips were black with dried blood, his eyes pink with zig-zaggy veins.

"I can do it myself," Wyatt said, rolling over and crawling for the shade. "I might be dying, but I'm not dead yet."

"And it's a good thing. I don't think I have the energy to dig a hole big enough to bury you in."

"I'm so glad you still have your winning sense of humor," he said.

"Maintaining humor in stressful situations is one of my greatest strengths, you know that."

"I was being sarcastic. I much prefer the silence to your shrilly voice and lame jokes."

"Shrilly voice?"

"Yes, shrilly."

"What does that even mean?"

"I can't recite the exact definition, but shrilly means nasally, high pitched, annoying, or something along those lines."

"Nasally, high pitched, and annoying, huh?"

"Mmm-hmm."

"Jeez, thanks, Wyatt. That's such a nice thing to say."

"I'm not trying to hurt your feelings. I'm just telling you the truth."

"You know what, enjoy the silence then," I said. "Me and my annoying voice are going for a walk."

"Don't be dumb."

"Oh, now I'm dumb?"

"I'm just saying, going for a walk all alone isn't the best idea. We should stay together."

"At this point, I don't even care. Facing the dangers of

the Outback beats sitting around here with you and your crummy attitude."

"Fine, don't listen to me."

"Fine, I won't."

"Don't get lost out there," Wyatt said.

"And don't you go dying on me," I shot back. "There's a long list of things I'd rather do today than watch buzzards pick you apart."

This actually got a laugh out of Wyatt.

"On that note, keep a look out for that huntsman I saw a few minutes ago," I added.

"Oh, yeah right. You think I'm going to fall for that?"

"I was going to spare you the horror, but now I could care less whether you're freaked out or not. It was crawling down that tree right behind you. All righty then, catch you later!"

At that, Wyatt jumped to his feet, brushed himself off and began to look around on the ground for the spider.

I chuckled to myself and kept on walking. Okay, I have to admit, I didn't walk far, only about 50 meters due west to a bluff overlooking the narrow river.

I found a smooth rock, sat down and searched the sky.

Come on rescue plane! Where the heck are you?

I looked everywhere.

There was no plane.

What I did see, perched on a high branch, was another sea eagle patiently scouting the area for prey. And across the murky river, a lone water buffalo moved along a steep eroded bank. Each time the buffalo took a step, the earth crumbled underneath its hoofs and it would slide closer to the water. It looked like the buffalo had come down the slope to the nearby billabong—which is a pool of stagnant water formed by the river—to take a drink and couldn't climb back up.

The river below was still, unmoving, like a green mirror. White clouds reflected on its surface. So stealthy was the crocodile floating toward the buffalo, I didn't even notice it until it was just offshore. When the buffalo spotted the croc, it panicked and tried to run up the sandy bluff, away from the water. The buffalo's frantic attempt to move away from the croc was actually bringing it closer, as more ground gave way under its hooves. I could hardly watch as the croc positioned itself, waiting for just the right moment to attack.

That moment came quickly.

It was unbelievable to see just how fast the croc shot from the water, like a bolt of lightning. Then came a loud *SNAP*! Just like that, the croc had the buffalo's hind leg trapped in its jaw. Fighting like mad, the buffalo bucked up and down and eventually pulled the croc completely out of the water. The croc had to be 15 feet long, maybe more, which showed just how powerful the water buffalo was. Though it tried with all its might, the buffalo couldn't get up and over the steep ledge. After a fierce battle, his strength was all but gone.

Slowly, painfully, the buffalo was dragged into the water. It was halfway under when it gave one last attempt to fight its way free. Twisting, lurching, thrashing. I almost thought it was going to break loose of the croc's grip, when a second crocodile shot out of nowhere and locked its jaw over the buffalo's nose. Together these two large crocs took the buffalo down. There was a tremendous thrashing at first, like a geyser erupting from underneath the river, then only a few ripples, and finally total stillness, as if nothing at all had happened.

Being an aspiring filmmaker, part of me wished I had a video camera with me. I mean, to capture such a dramatic spectacle, as sad as it was, well, that's what the best nature filmmakers do. At the same time, a big part of me was glad I didn't have a camera. Because, to tell the truth, that was a scene I really don't need to see again.

WYATT

MARCH 17, 3:51 PM
OUTBACK
105° FAHRENHEIT, 41° CELSIUS
WIND: 5-10 MPH
SKIES: PARTLY CLOUDY

Gannon and I have had a few arguments today. It is only natural, given our stressful predicament, but if I am being truthful with myself, I'd have to say that I'm more to blame for our fights than he is. Earlier today I was worn out and not feeling well at all and wound up saying some very unnecessary things to my brother. I only realized this after Gannon stormed off. For him to leave camp and go off into the

Outback alone, as big of a chicken as he can be, I knew he must have been fuming. At that moment, I was angry with him, too, and decided not to follow. After ten or so minutes passed, I regretted my decision. If something happened to him, I'd never forgive myself. The longer he was gone, the more I worried, and that worry brought to light the things I said that I shouldn't have.

No need for me to go into the details. I'm sure Gannon has already written about it in his journal. What's important is that he returned safely. I was so happy when I saw him come back up the muddy hill toward me, I ran down to meet him. To have tension between you and someone you care about is a terrible feeling.

The first thing I did was apologize. Gannon listened patiently and finally accepted my apology. I was relieved. We were a team again, and remaining a team is critical to our survival.

We went back up the hill, sat down under the hibiscus and Gannon told me about a water buffalo he'd just seen pulled down by two large crocodiles. This brought to mind what Darla had told us about how far inland some crocodiles wander at night. A few kilometers, she had said. That's just under two miles, and we've never been more than a half-mile from the river. If a hungry croc finds us tonight, how are we going to protect ourselves? I don't think Pete's rifle is powerful enough to stop a full-sized crocodile. I suppose it gives us a chance, at least.

Oh, how I dread nightfall.

We better get going. There's enough light left to cover some more ground before dark. Pete is out there somewhere and we're committed to do all we can to find him.

GANNON

MARCH 17,
ALMOST NIGHTTIME, I.E. ALMOST MOSSIE,
SNAKE, AND MIMI TIME

As good as our latest shelter is, and it's probably the best one we've built, Wyatt and I haven't figured out how to make it completely waterproof. It might just be the power of these torrential storms. The rain out here comes down in buckets, sometimes with wind so strong that it blows the rain sideways. By the time the rain stops, Wyatt and I are waterlogged and shivering. If it's still daytime, we set out in search of sunlight and warmth. When we find it, we plop down on the ground and let the sun speed the drying because hiking in soggy clothes has rubbed rashes on our legs and under our arms and we don't want them to get worse. These moments of relative comfort are only temporary, as soon after a storm the air becomes unbelievably hot and humid and the bugs return.

Actually, that's another problem we haven't figured out, how to keep the bugs from biting. Is there a natural bug repellent out here? I wish I knew, because the mosquitos and other biting insects are feasting on any exposed skin.

I'm telling you, they have a real fondness for my blood. Took only a day in the bush to realize what an idiot I was to buy shorts and a short sleeve shirt! I mean, seriously, what was I thinking? Wyatt is doing a lot better with his "head to toe coverage." He has some bites, sure, but not nearly as many as I do. To give an idea of just how many bug bites I have, I stopped counting the welts on my arms, legs, and face when I reached 100, and I wasn't close to finished.

Apart from being famished, something else is going on. My muscles and joints are achy, and my energy seems to be fading with the setting sun. It'll be dark soon, and there's another storm moving this way. We have plenty of fresh water, but it has been hard to endure the rigors of our trek without food. Pretty soon, we need to find something substantial to eat. I know there is food all around us. Other than the hibiscus flower, we're just not sure what's edible and what's poisonous and don't want to take the risk until it's our absolute last option.

WYATT

MARCH 17, 9:43 PM
90° FAHRENHEIT, 32° CELSIUS
WIND: 5-10 MPH
SKIES: LIGHT RAIN

Another day has passed. Still no sign of Pete. Not even a trace. No sign of a rescue plane either. No sign of anyone.

I very much regret leaving camp to search for him. No, I

shouldn't say that, I don't regret searching for Pete. I regret the fact that we got lost in the process. That was a hasty decision, made out of fear that Pete was in trouble after he wandered from camp, but we should have taken more time to mark our camp before we ran off after him.

Of course, Gannon and I want to do all we can to find him, and we are, but it seems more likely that all three of us will perish as a result. We have discussed trying to trek back to the wreckage, as that seems the most likely place to be rescued, but I don't know that we'd ever find it. If we couldn't find our way back the first day, how could we possibly do it now, after several days trekking through the bush?

It is easy to understand how someone can get lost out here and never be found, just like Ludwig Leichardt. Instead of dwelling on the obvious, we're trying to keep our minds occupied with what needs to be done, from one hour to the next, just to survive.

Not long ago, Gannon crawled into the shelter to lie down.

"I'm so hungry," he said faintly and closed his eyes. "Hopefully a rescue will come tomorrow. It has to, right, Wyatt?"

"I hope so."

Gannon rolled over on his side and was asleep almost immediately.

I spent another 45 minutes placing an extra layer of paper tree bark over the top of our shelter. I ate a few more flowers, too, but that won't sustain us much longer. I've had my fill, yet still my stomach growls and my body hungers for nutrients. Our time is running out. We need to find Pete. We need to find a village, a farm, a home, something . . . anything.

GANNON
4TH DAY, I THINK, STILL EARLY
SUNBURNED, WET, AND BUG BITTEN

No question. Something is definitely attacking my system. Woke in the middle of the night feeling nauseous, tingly in places, numb in others. This tragic expedition has taken a toll. I'm exhausted, hungry, scared, soaking wet half the day, boiling hot the other, and my legs, arms, and face are all swollen from the bug bites. Oh, and let's not forget, we were just in a plane crash and our pilot Pete is missing and probably dead.

I suppose there aren't many people who would feel normal in this situation. I'm just worried that this is something far more serious.

For now, I'm staying in our shelter. More rest is the only thing I can manage.

WYATT

Last night was uneventful. No crocs wandered into camp. No dingoes. No snakes or spiders either. At least, none that I saw.

This morning the rain passed and a breeze carried cool air through camp. Cooler than we've felt since being stranded, at least by a few degrees. I stayed under the tree for a while, unmoving, enjoying the breeze, which was soothing against my sunburnt face. A koala even paid a visit, climbing a nearby eucalyptus tree to eat some leaves and take a nap. To see this animal, so secure in its natural habitat, was comforting. It gave me hope.

However, there is still our reality to contend with. The heat is relentless, as are the bugs. The only breaks from the sun and bugs come from the spectacular thunderstorms that engulf the land. Again, there are clouds on the horizon. Big and white, like a bushel of cotton, with darker shades of gray at the bottom. It's been four days since our crash, and three days since Pete disappeared. I'm wondering how he is faring.

Today we must gather more food. Fishing does not seem to be an option. Gannon said he's not going near the water after seeing the buffalo taken by the crocs, and neither am I.

It's just too dangerous in this area. Since eating the Vegemite sandwiches, we've been living off flower petals and are desperately in need of more calories. Protein and vitamins, too. Some kind of meat or bird eggs would be our best bet.

A koala bear napping in a tree

Gannon was up a lot last night, so he's still sleeping. Tried for a while to rouse him. He finally woke, said he couldn't even think of hiking and that he needs more sleep.

Afraid I have no choice. I have to hunt.

WYATT

MARCH 18, 2:32 PM
100° FAHRENHEIT, 38° CELSIUS
WIND: 0 MPH

After wandering for a couple of hours, all the while being careful not to lose sight of the high rock spire that is near last night's camp, I spotted a kangaroo. Decent-size. Enough meat to last a few days.

I swallowed hard, lifted Pete's rifle to my shoulder, and clicked off the safety. The kangaroo, unaware that a rifle was fixed on it, stood perfectly still in a clearing. I felt a bead of sweat run down my face as I placed my index finger over the trigger. I knew I only had a few seconds before the kangaroo noticed me and went for cover.

I had to take a shot.

I had to pull the trigger.

Do it, pull the trigger, I told myself.

GO ON, PULL IT!

As I applied pressure to the trigger, a baby joey raised its head from the kangaroo's pouch. Quickly, I lowered the rifle.

My movements must have made a noise, because suddenly the mother kangaroo noticed me and hopped away.

I continued to search for a few hours more and did see three other kangaroos, but they were too far off and I never again had the opportunity or desire to take a shot. I did not find much else. I even climbed a number of trees to look into bird's nests for eggs, but they were all empty. In the last tree, I saw a huntsman spider skittering across a branch toward me, and became so stricken with fear I almost lost my grip and fell to the ground. No more climbing trees for me.

Right now, I am back at our camp with Gannon, empty handed, hungry, and fatigued. Need to lie down. Need to conserve energy.

GANNON

OUTBACK, WHERE ELSE . . .

I have been so lethargic and achy with a stiff neck and fever and whatnot and it's not that I am feeling better or anything, but I'm suddenly having this strange and particularly lucid moment, and feel the need to make some quick notes.

See, I've had a nagging thought going round and round in my head all day. I have tried to shake it, to put it out of my mind, but I just can't. The thought I'm having, I guess it's more of a feeling, actually, is that my life is about to be cut short.

This is not an exaggeration. All of the signs point to death. My mouth is bone dry. My tongue is like a strip of sandpaper. My face is burnt to oblivion, peeled and bleeding in places, and I am swollen from bug bites all over my body. I'm hot and then cold and then hot again. I'm unsteady and my hands tremble. The words I'm writing now are almost impossible to read.

I have been sick before, very sick at times, but I have never felt quite this bad. This is something different. I don't know what, I just have an unsettled feeling that something is going haywire inside of me and that whatever it is could very well be the beginning of the end.

WYATT

MARCH 18, 6:47 PM
89° FAHRENHEIT, 32° CELSIUS

What woke me from a dead sleep was the sensation of something moving over my right arm and onto my stomach. I held still and kept my eyes closed, afraid of what I might find. When I finally mustered the courage to open my eyes, a narrow tongue lapped at my face.

A snake!

And not just *any* snake. An eastern brown!

I was sure of the species, having chased one away from

our camp the first day. I also knew that if this snake were to strike me I'd be dead within the hour.

I held my breath as the eastern brown slithered slowly over the top of me. Other than opening my eyes, I did not dare move. If I could keep from startling the snake, or causing it to feel threatened, it might not feel the need to strike.

The snake was solid brown in color. No more than four feet, it was thicker in the middle and very thin at the tail. The snake's eyes were solid black. It stopped and looked right at me. Its forked tongue flicked and disappeared.

I had to breathe, and did so by inhaling extremely slowly to keep my stomach from rising too abruptly.

How quickly would a bite to the face kill me? Most likely within minutes.

The snake moved down the left side of my body and onto the ground, away from Gannon, who was lying to my right. Finally, the eastern brown had separated itself completely from me. For several more minutes, I held perfectly still. Once the snake was outside the shelter and beyond striking distance, I rolled over, got to my knees and crawled out to see where it was going.

Grabbing my camera from my pack, I zoomed in from a safe distance and snapped a few photos. The snake continued moving further away from camp. Eventually feeling comfortable with its distance, I staggered back to the shelter and sat down. Fortunately, Gannon had slept through the whole thing. If he had woken up and panicked, the snake might have struck us both. Inspecting the markings in the sand, it appeared the eastern brown had crawled right over him, too. Gannon had not even noticed. He was out, as still as a corpse.

Hold on! Had Gannon been bitten?

I went cold with fear.

Frantically, I checked his pulse and put my finger under his nose to make sure he was breathing. His heartbeat was strong, and I could feel warm air coming from his nostrils. Then I checked his legs and arms thoroughly for fang marks. I also checked his neck and face. His entire body is covered with red, welted bug bites, but I saw no sign of a snake bite. As I moved around him, he stirred.

"What are you doing?" he said, groggily.

"Nothing, just checking to make sure you're okay."

"I've felt better," he said and rolled over. "We need to eat, Wyatt. We need food."

An appetite, no sign of fang marks anywhere, clear speech, all of these things led me to believe that the snake had let him be. I relaxed and Gannon went back to sleep.

Outside, heat. White-blue sky overhead, streaks of orange on the horizon. Storms to the north. Occasional thunder and the low buzz of insects. Other than that, silence. We are alone. No one is near.

This is my third journal entry today, an unusual amount of writing to complete during a day of expedition. However, with little else to do, I am compelled to document every detail of our doomed adventure. It almost feels as if I am writing the last chapter of my life story, and maybe that of my brother, as well.

What happens next, I do not want to consider.

The deadly eastern brown snake

GANNON

LATE NIGHT

The passing hours are now made up of somewhat deliri-ous semiconscious moments, flashes of clarity, followed by sudden exhaustion and more sleep. It repeats just like that, over and over. Maybe this is my body's way of doing what it can to preserve life. I drank some rain we collected, but have eaten nothing in some time.

That's all I can write . . . just too tired.

WYATT
MARCH 19, 7:42 AM

There will be no hunt today.

Last night we were ambushed by dingoes. To protect ourselves, I was forced to use all of the bullets.

I fired several shots straight into the air when I first noticed the pack closing in on us. Gannon was still in the shelter. I yelled his name and warned him of the threat.

The dingoes were circling, getting nearer with each pass. I fired another shot into the air and put the rifle to my shoulder. The warning shots were not scaring them away. They were determined, growling, yelping, howling like mad! Gannon crawled out of the shelter and tore away a large stick from its frame. No sooner had he said he'd help me fight them off, than one of the dingoes charged, a large muscular male, not much smaller than a wolf. I quickly took aim and fired. The bullet hit a few inches in front of the dingo, spraying dirt and rock in its face. Luckily, that was enough to startle it. The dingo turned and raced off into the darkness. Gannon yelled something that I couldn't make out. Seconds later, another dingo came at me from behind. Hearing it snarl, I spun around and fired, missing again. Maybe it was the flash of light or the loud explosion from the barrel, but this dingo, too, altered its path and disappeared into the trees. A third dingo came from the left, toward Gannon. He swung the big stick at it like a sword, and the skittish dingo turned and ran.

If they all mount a charge at once, I thought, we won't stand a chance. I needed to prevent that from happening. I needed to go from being the prey, to being the predator.

"Get back in the shelter, Gannon! Now!"

"Why?"

"I'm going to shoot at anything that moves and I don't want to shoot you by accident."

Without another word, Gannon tossed the stick aside and dove into the shelter.

Keeping my finger on the trigger, I turned slowly, squinting into the darkness. The campfire I had built lit the eyes of an approaching dingo, maybe 40 feet away. I cracked off two shots in quick succession —*Boom-Boom!* I heard the bullets rip through the leaves. The dingo turned and darted off, the animal's whimper fading as it moved away from camp. Maybe I had hit it. Everything was happening so fast, I couldn't tell. To my left, I heard a rustle, turned and immediately fired at a shadow moving through the bushes. This time, I heard a yelp. It sounded like there were more dingoes in those shrubs, so

I fired a second, third, and fourth shot into them. When I pulled the trigger a fifth time, it clicked.

I pulled it again.

Click.

One more time.

Another click.

I was out of bullets!

I stood, panting nervously. Turning my ears slowly to the darkness on all sides, I listened for any indication that we were still surrounded, even the most subtle snap of a twig. I half expected the dingoes to mount a full-scale assault of our camp at any second, to overtake us and tear us to shreds. But the Outback was quiet. The dingoes, it appeared, had left.

This morning I combed the area around camp and did not find a single dead or wounded dingo, so I must not have hit any. If I had, we could have cooked and eaten the meat. That alone might have been enough to keep us alive for another week.

Instead, we face a grim reality. Gannon is still inside the shelter, shivering with fever. He was brave to come out and fight in his condition, and I admire him for that. I am just afraid the stress of it may have done him in. It's possible that I may hold out a few more days, but without food, I cannot travel any further. We have refilled our canteens with rainwater, but our chances of finding enough food to sustain us are slim. However, I will give it every last thing I've got to do so.

Otherwise, I am certain our expedition will end like the expeditions of Burke, Willsinsert a comma and Leichardt.

GANNON

I woke from a state of unconsciousness without the ability to move or to even open my eyes and was only partially aware of who or where I was.

Colors morphed behind my eyelids, blues and greens and purples. My brain suddenly tuned into my breathing, the way it came and went through my mouth, how it moved over my dry, cracked tongue, the sensation of my lungs expanding and retracting. Breathing is probably the most basic, taken-for-granted, yet critical function we undertake on a moment-to-moment basis and to be aware of it was everything. It meant I was still alive.

Where was Pete? I wondered.

Had he been rescued?

Was he leading a search for us?

Or was he face down in the Outback, vultures circling overhead?

I didn't really have the desire or strength to ponder these terrible thoughts and lucky for me they faded almost as if they had been taken away by the wind. I listened to my heartbeat. It had slowed considerably. A strange peace came over me. There was no doubt in my mind, I had begun my journey into the ever after.

Then, somewhere nearby, I heard a different sort of sound. A sound like I had never heard.

I wiped dirt away from my eyes and tried to blink. Though there were no tears left to cleanse them, I managed to pry my eyes open just a sliver. Turning my head to the right, I looked beyond the shelter. A grainy image of Wyatt came into partial focus. He was sitting up, about 30 or so feet away, staring off into the distance. I rubbed my eyes again and slowly turned my head to see what he was looking at.

What I saw were trees and shrubs, all out of focus, and a hazy light on the horizon. Nothing more.

My head fell back into the dirt.

The sound came once more, a low and ambient tone, a sound that seemed almost to blend with the landscape. What on earth makes such a sound? Were these voices I was hearing? Voices from the afterlife?

Blinking again and again, my sight began to clear, at least, just enough to make out what was standing before me.

It was a person!

Wait a sec, I thought. A person? Couldn't be, could it?

"Pete?" I said.

There was no response.

Was I seeing things? Was this a hallucination? Or maybe I was dead already? In such a state of delirium, I couldn't figure out what was going on.

The figure came closer. I blinked and wiped my eyes again. It wasn't just one person. It was two. Two people were walking toward me, silhouetted against the horizon, whispering to one another in a foreign language.

Feeling faint, I fell back into the dirt. When I opened my eyes again, the two people were standing just outside the shelter. They were teenagers, a boy and a girl, Aboriginals. The boy was shirtless, wearing only dark green shorts worn thin and frayed around the bottom. He had curly dark hair and held a long, thin branch carved into a sharp point at the end. The girl wore a red t-shirt and brown pants cut off at the knees. Her hair was shoulder length and wavy, auburn in color, but lighter at the tips. They both had sandals on their feet.

One of them said something I didn't understand, so I just started talking.

"My name's Gannon," I said, my voice scratchy. "My brother and I need help."

They looked at one another, then back to me.

"Our plane crashed and we've been stranded in the Outback. We haven't had any food in days. We're desperate."

They stared without saying a word.

"You don't understand anything I'm saying, do you?" I said.

Again the boy and girl looked at one another.

"We understand every single word of it, mate," the boy said.

Oh my gosh! They spoke English!

It felt like I'd taken an electric shock to the heart. Life once again pulsed through me! We had been found!

"Try this," the boy said, reaching into a satchel and handing me something, a root or a strip of jerky, it didn't really matter. It was food! I tore into it so ravenously I nearly ripped out my front teeth.

"Oh, my gosh. Thank you so much!" I said, chewing vigorously on what tasted like some kind of cured meat.

"Forgive us for our silence," the boy said. "We're just a little shocked that we found you alive."

"So you were looking for us?" I asked.

"A few days ago we heard on the radio that a plane had recently gone down somewhere in the Outback. My sister had seen a plane fly overhead the day before, so she convinced our parents to let us go on a walkabout. What she really wanted to do was look for you. And so did I."

"Since there was no mayday call everyone assumed you were dead," she said. "They said there were three people in the plane. Is that right?"

"Yes, that's right."

"The pilot, Pete, he was injured and we think he went looking for help, but we haven't seen him since."

Wyatt staggered over to us.

"This is my brother, Wyatt," I said.

The boy reached into his satchel, retrieved another strip of meat and handed it to him.

Wyatt thanked him and tore off a bite.

"You were flying over restricted air space," the girl said.

"Really?" I said. "Pete thought he might have been."

"You're in Arnhem Land," the boy said. "That's another reason no one has found you. Since there are no commercial flights in this area, they're looking for you in Kakadu."

"We're so sorry," I said. "Really, we mean no disrespect. We honestly didn't even know we were in Arnhem Land."

"I'm sure Pete meant no harm by it," Wyatt said. "I think he accidentally drifted off course. Either way, like my brother said, we're very sorry. We just need help. Gannon's been sick and we need to find Pete. He's probably in worse shape than us."

The brother and sister looked at one another, then back to Wyatt and me.

"Do not worry," the boy said. "We are here to help you. Do you know which way the pilot walked?"

"Unfortunately, we don't have a clue," I said.

"He had a bad concussion and probably wasn't sure where he was going himself," Wyatt added. "We've just been follow-ing the easiest path through the bush, hoping we'd find him."

"Are you both well enough to hike?" the girl asked.

"I am," Wyatt said. "How about you, Gannon?"

"I don't know," I said, wondering how I would actually manage a lengthy Outback trek. "If we go really slow, maybe."

"Grab your belongings and follow us," the boy instructed. "We will look for signs of the pilot as we walk."

"Oh, one more thing," I said, not yet ready to stand. "You wouldn't happen to know a brother and sister named Darla and Roman?"

"We do," the boy said. "They grew up not too far from our village."

"They were our guides in Kakadu," Wyatt said. "We had plans to meet up with them again and go search for prehistoric fossils."

"We will track them down when we get to the village," the girl said. "I can hardly wait to tell them we have found you alive!"

"Yeah, me too!" my brother said. "We also need to get in touch with my parents somehow."

"Our uncle will be able to help you," the boy said. "He operates the emergency radios. Let's be on our way."

Still lying on the ground, I finished the strip of meat and chugged down several gulps of the rainwater we'd collected, while Wyatt went about gathering our backpacks, journals, and Pete's rifle with no more bullets. The reality of being found had jolted me back to life, but the world around me was still moving in slow motion. When I finally stood and took a step, my legs buckled underneath me and I crumbled to the ground. Wyatt dropped everything and ran to my side.

"Are you okay?" he asked.

"That I can move at all is something of a miracle to me," I said, "but I think I need some more rest before I can go anywhere."

"Some more food probably wouldn't hurt either," the girl said.

"I could eat an entire water buffalo by myself," I said.

"We were thinking of something that's a little easier to catch," the boy said, "but we'll see."

"You know, we didn't even get your names," Wyatt said, extending his hand to the girl.

"My name is Yindi," the girl said. "And this is my brother, Toba."

"Just curious, do your names have a meaning?" I asked.

"Yes, Yindi means the sun. But I don't know what Toba means."

She turned to her brother.

"I don't know what it means either," Toba said. "Maybe Mom and Dad just liked the sound of it."

Everyone laughed.

"Okay, time for some more food," Toba said, shaking his pointer finger. "I'll be back soon."

At that, he set off, and boy am I relieved! I mean, food is on the way! A real meal! Nutrition! Calories! We've been saved!

I just hope we can now do the same for Pete and get back to the village safely. Okay, so, Yindi, Wyatt, and I just discussed the plan. If my energy returns and there's any remaining sunlight after we get some more food in our bellies, the search will continue!

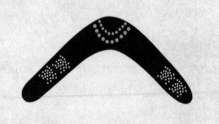

PART III

THE WALKABOUT

WYATT

MARCH 19, 7:58 PM
ARNHEM LAND
91° FAHRENHEIT, 33° CELSIUS
WIND: 0-5 MPH

A plump iguana roasted on the fire.

Not over the fire, twirling on a spit. It was in the fire, lying right on top of the burning wood. Nose to tail, it had to be four feet long.

"Once the skin turns black, the meat is good to eat," Toba said. "Tender and juicy."

Gannon leaned over to me and whispered, his voice still sounding parched and weak.

"I think the only thing less appetizing than a Vegemite sandwich might be a big, fat, scaly lizard."

"Are you really going to be picky at this point?" I asked.

Gannon stared at the iguana and thought for a moment. "I guess not."

Fact is, I couldn't be happier to have Gannon showing signs of his old self. He looks thin, frail even, and his sluggishness remains, but his sense of humor has returned. That's a sign that he is feeling stronger. Toba thinks Gannon may have had Dengue fever, which you get from mosquitos. Symptoms are similar to what Gannon experienced—fever, nausea, headaches, fatigue, etc.—but it takes up to two weeks for Dengue symptoms to show and we haven't been in the Outback that long, so we're really not sure what made him sick. My guess would be that the trauma of the crash, coupled with Gannon's numerous insect bites and extended lack of food wound up compromising his immune system.

The iguana's skin eventually blackened, as promised. Lifting the hefty lizard with a long stick, Yindi moved it atop a rock and flipped it onto its back. Then Toba used the tip of his spear to slice into the side of the lizard's belly. Underneath the charred skin was bright white meat.

Toba cut out chunks of the meat and passed them around. I was so hungry I could have cared less what it tasted like. It was protein, which my body craved, so I didn't hesitate for a second before throwing it into my mouth.

"Whoa-whoa-whoa-hot," I said, fanning my mouth with my hand. I chewed it a few quick times, swallowed and felt the burn as it slid down my throat.

Gannon studied the iguana meat in his hand.

"Go ahead," I said. "It's really good."

"I'm just waiting for it to cool," he said.

Toba handed me another strip. Steam rose off the top. I blew on it a few times, then a few more, and finally tossed it back.

Gannon nibbled on his piece of meat like a bird.

"Just eat it, Gannon," I said. "We were about to starve out here, you were sick, I thought we were goners. Now, we've been rescued, you're feeling better, and we have a hot meal in front of us. This is cause for celebration!"

"All right, all right," Gannon said. "Here goes nothing!"

Tilting his head back, he dropped the full piece of meat into his mouth and chewed vigorously.

"Good, isn't it?" Yindi asked.

"I can't believe I'm about to say this, but iguana is delicious!"

Each of us laughed and kept eating until the lizard had been picked clean of meat. After our meal, we were all full and sat around watching the fire for a while without saying much.

I was mostly wondering about Pete. We have found nothing since we left our original camp, not even a clue. Where could he have gone? What has happened to him? Here we are, safe with Toba and Yindi, our stomachs full, and yet, the whereabouts of Pete is still unknown. If he hasn't been found by someone else, he must be suffering terribly, if he's even still alive.

I also felt sorry for my parents, assuming they had received word by now that our plane was missing. Imagining my mom and dad sick with worry, it made my stomach turn.

"Would anyone like dessert?" Toba asked, taking my mind away from Pete and my parents.

"If it's something else we have to kill," Gannon said, "I'll pass."

"No killing involved," Toba said, laughing. "We just have to find it, and I've spotted a guide that can lead us there."

Toba stood up and slowly moved away from the fire. His arms were extended. His eyes locked on something. Then, like a shot, he clasped his hands together and walked back to the fire.

"What did you catch?" I asked.

"A honey bee," he said.

Toba carefully handed the bee to his sister, pulled a flower from a tree, and tore off a petal.

"What's he doing?" Gannon asked.

"You'll see," Yindi said.

Toba then pulled away a strip of bark from a hibiscus, tore off a string as thin as a fishing line, and walked back to Yindi. With the delicate touch of a surgeon, the two of them tied the string to the bee and attached the pink flower petal to the line.

"Gannon, do you think you can walk now?" Toba asked.

"I think so," my brother answered.

Slowly, Gannon stood, placing his hand atop a rock to help lift his weight. Fully upright, he took a deep breath, exhaled, and walked around in a small circle, stretching out his arms as he moved.

"Yeah, I think I can manage a short walk," Gannon said.

"That's great," Toba replied. "Grab your things. We're going to follow this little guy."

Toba then let the bee fly away, easily carrying the petal along with it. Yindi waved us on, as Toba tracked the floating petal deeper into the woods.

"The bee will lead us to the hive," Yindi said. "Follow us if you would like some honey."

"Oh my gosh, that's so cool!" Gannon said.

We had been walking for about ten minutes when I noticed a buzzing sound. Built into the split of a large tree was a massive hive of bees. As if immune to bee stings, Toba walked right up to the hive and began to saw away at the honeycomb with his spear. The rest of us kept our distance from the swarming bees. When Toba turned around, he held a large piece of honeycomb.

"Dessert is served," he said.

"Aren't the bees stinging you?" Gannon asked.

"I got a few stings. Nothing bad. If I wasn't so impatient, I could have built a little fire and smoked them out. But it's getting dark, so I figured we should get right to the honey and give ourselves enough time to set up camp."

Toba handed out chunks of honeycomb, and we each immediately sank our teeth into them. The golden honey was deliciously sweet and dripped down our chins. I remember reading that it takes 60,000 bees to gather nectar from some 2 million flowers just to make one pound of honey. That's a tremendous amount of work and made me feel almost guilty for devouring the honey so quickly. However, the guilt didn't last long. The honey was simply too good!

GANNON
ALMOST DREAM TIME

By the time we'd finished our surprisingly tasty feast of iguana, cooked medium-well, and sticky, sweet honeycomb fresh from the hive, it was nearly dark.

As we gathered wood for the fire and went about building two simple shelters for the night, I shouted Pete's name several more times, my hands cupped over my mouth to amplify the sound.

"PEEEEETE!"

There was no response.

I try to remain hopeful, I really do, but at this point, I almost don't expect to find him. We aren't giving up, though, that's for sure! I'll shout his name several more times before I lie down for the night and tomorrow I'll do it all the way back to the village, but that's about all we can do.

As night fell, Toba and Yindi explained that the sort of hunting and gathering we had done today was an example of how Aboriginals had lived for tens of thousands of years, but that it's no longer necessary, since today they have a grocery store in their village. Even as they adapt to modern comforts, their grandfather, a respected elder named Jarli, encourages hunting and gathering as part of their upbringing. He says it's important to learn the old ways. Apparently, Jarli is the one who convinced Toba and Yindi's father to let them go on a walkabout, and thank goodness for that!

"Even though life is changing around the world," Toba said, "we need to maintain our connection with the land and nature. My grandfather asks us, 'What if tomorrow the store has no food? What do you do then?' Besides, the old ways are healthier, he says, and he is right. The food from the grocery store may taste good, but it is not always good for your body. After living off the land and eating the same food for many thousands of years, it is hard for us to adapt to a different way of life and a different diet."

"Jarli says we cannot know our culture or ourselves without an intimate knowledge of the land and its history," Yindi added.

"Our generation is growing up with televisions and computers and video games and all these things," Toba continued, "but the elders are trying to keep our culture strong for the sake of future generations. They do not want the old ways to be forgotten."

I was happy to hear it. I mean, after all, we're talking about the oldest culture in the world. Tens of thousands of years of wisdom and knowledge, an entire civilization of thoughts and dreams. If the Aboriginal culture were to disappear from this earth, it would be an absolute tragedy!

"Toba, you and I are on the same page," I said, excited. "I want to learn more. I want to learn about your creation stories and Dreamtime and songlines! I want to write it all down so that it can be shared with kids all over the world!"

"Many of our Dreamtime stories are sacred and aren't to be shared with others. They are just for our people to know and to pass down to our children."

"Oh, I see."

"But our grandfather is a great storyteller and can explain the songlines better than anyone," Yindi said. "Maybe he will be willing to share some of his knowledge with you."

"So we'll get to meet him?" I asked.

"Absolutely. As soon as we get to the village."

"Oh, and one more small request," I said. "There wouldn't happen to be anyone in your village who can show me how to play the didgeridoo, would there?"

"Again, that would be my grandfather," Toba said. "He is very good and I'm sure he'd be happy to give you a lesson."

"Wow, that would be great!"

Yindi says we're another full day's walk from the village. And Toba mentioned having to make a shallow river crossing along the way. Sounds a little sketchy, if you ask me, but hey, we're with a couple of Outback experts, so I'm not too worried. If all goes well, we should arrive at the village tomorrow by sundown.

On the whole, I'd say things are looking up. Compared to just yesterday, way, way up. But still, and please excuse the pun, we are not out of the *woods* yet!

WYATT

MARCH 20, 11:04 AM
ARNHEM LAND
93° FAHRENHEIT, 34° CELSIUS
WIND: 5-10 MPH
SKIES: CLOUDY

A booming storm halted our trek midmorning.

"Namarrgon seems a little angry today," Gannon said, as we crowded into a narrow cave.

"Ah, you know about Lightning Man, do you?" Toba asked.

"Yes, Roman taught us."

A clap of thunder rumbled so powerfully I could feel the vibration under my feet.

"Whoa," Gannon said. "I've never felt thunder like that before."

"Namarrgon is just having fun with us," Yindi said. "The skies are clear to the north. This will soon pass."

Yindi was right. The storm flashed and boomed for

another 20 minutes and was gone. Once the skies had settled, we moved out. The rocks were pooled with water, the soil soggy and slippery. Our boots sank into the muck with each step. Every 50 to 100 feet, we all called Pete's name. Near a glade of eucalyptus trees, we heard rustling and for the quickest of moments I was hopeful that it was him making his way to us through the brush. What emerged instead was a huge water buffalo. It stopped and stared us down from about 75 feet away. We stopped too. When it lowered its head, I thought it was about to charge. But Toba made a whooping noise and waved his spear, and very casually the water buffalo turned and trotted off.

Charging water buffalo

Soon after, we made a short stop to rest our legs and hydrate while Yindi gathered some "bush tucker," which is basically anything in the Outback that's edible. With a side-arm chuck, she flung her boomerang up into the trees, aiming at a section of high hanging fruit. Several fell, hitting the ground with a thud.

"She sure is good with that boomerang," I said to Toba.

"Probably the best shot in the village," he said. "She could knock a bird out of the sky midflight, if she had to."

Yindi picked up the fruits and continued on, gathering a few more from lower branches. Within a couple minutes she returned with her hands full of what she said were cluster figs and kakadu plums, both of which were juicy and delicious.

It's about time to continue on our way. From our current location, we are only three or four hours from the village. Truth be told, I've nearly lost all hope of finding Pete, and that is a heavy thought to carry. It brings me some relief to know that we will be in touch with our parents soon. At least their nightmare will be over.

GANNON

East Alligator River

Sometime early afternoon we came to the river Yindi had mentioned. Pausing to gaze across this wide stretch of dark water sent chills down my spine. Just below the surface, bona fide man-eaters were almost definitely waiting in ambush.

"You know, I was hoping the river wasn't so wide," I said.

At the most narrow point, I'd say the river was about the length of a football field, probably 300 feet across, if not more.

"And the rock crossing you mentioned," Wyatt added, "I assumed it was above water."

The rocks that stretched from one side of the river to the other were gathered at the top of a small waterfall that cascaded about seven or eight feet into deeper water. Problem was, the rocks had a couple of inches of water flowing over the top of them, which meant that they were slippery.

"Are you sure there's no way to go around this river?" I asked. "I mean, I feel like there must be a dozen crocs in there just waiting for something to cross."

"The rocks were above water when we crossed a couple of days ago," Toba said. "The rains have raised the river. But the water flowing over the rocks is very shallow. So is the water upriver for at least another 30 meters. If there was a croc on the high side of the rock crossing, we would be able to see it."

Toba shielded his eyes with his hand and scanned the area.

"I don't see any, do you?" he asked.

We all surveyed the water above the falls.

"Looks clear to me," Wyatt said.

"We'll be just fine as long as no one slips and goes over the falls. On the low side of the river, it's like you say, Gannon. There are probably crocs."

"And I bet right now they're licking their chops," I said.

This got a laugh out of Toba.

"Just don't slip," he said. "Okay, stay close behind me."

At that, Toba stepped out onto the first rock, then moved

to a second, and a third. He made it look easy. Maybe it wouldn't be so difficult after all, right?

Wrong!

Wyatt slipped on the first rock and went down hard, falling upriver thankfully, and into very shallow water. He jumped to his feet quickly, more embarrassed than anything. Still, his fall had proven just how dangerous this crossing could be. Slip and tumble downriver and you'd likely find yourself in a world of trouble.

Toba came back to Wyatt and held his backpack while Wyatt gathered himself.

"Let me take this for you," Toba said, slinging the pack over his shoulders.

"That's okay," Wyatt said. "I can carry it."

"I insist. I've crossed this river many, many times. Since this is your first crossing, it will be easier if you go without the added weight."

"Just step slowly," Yindi said, moving onto the rocks behind Wyatt. "Do not transfer your weight to the front leg until you know you have a solid footing."

"Okay," Wyatt said. "I think I got it."

Toba moved ahead and we all followed. There was literally no more than an inch or two of water flowing over the rocks. "I can do this," I said to myself, and put my arms out to the side for balance. "Just take it slow and steady."

Step by careful step, we moved across. Toba and Yindi were quite comfortable, looking more or less like they were strolling down a sidewalk. Wyatt and I, on the other hand, looked like we were walking on a tightrope.

I kept my eyes on the rocks, totally focused, and before I knew it we were almost halfway across! Looking over the falls, I examined the water below. No sign of a croc anywhere. No bubbles, no floating eyeballs staring at us, no spiny tail slithering in our direction. This was reassuring. I mean, if I'd seen one rise to the surface, it might have been enough to make me lose my balance and fall right into its open jaws. Instead, the water looked peaceful. My confidence grew. This is totally doable, I thought. We're going to make it!

As I studied the rocks before me, searching for my next step, I was startled by a frightened gasp and looked up just in time to see a big splash in the river below.

A second later, Wyatt popped up at the base of the falls, his arms flailing. Terrified, I screamed my brother's name. Toba searched frantically for a place where Wyatt might be able to climb back up. The rocks where he was treading water were rounded and smooth and covered with algae. Add to that the force of the falls and the climbing out seemed nearly impossible. But what other choice was there? He had to get out of the river, and he tried, pulling himself up a few feet before slipping and splashing back into the river.

The thought of what could happen to my brother at any moment made me go numb. I scanned the surface of the water. Fortunately, the river around him was calm. I didn't spot a single croc. I saw nothing at all, actually. Maybe he'd get lucky!

Toba had moved ahead about 50 feet and was yelling Wyatt's name and pointing to an area where the waterfall parted. In this section of the falls, there were several rocks stacked atop one another, like smooth steps, only they were dry. Without having to swim all the way to shore, which was easily another 100+ feet away, climbing these rocks appeared to be Wyatt's best shot.

"Quick, swim here!" Toba said, waving his arms. "I can help you up!"

Wyatt took off like an Olympian. Toba climbed down part of the way and positioned himself to hoist Wyatt up. This short swim seemed to unfold in slow motion.

"Come on, Wyatt," I was whispering to myself. "Get there . . . get there!"

He was maybe halfway to Toba when a crocodile rose to the surface between them! I tried to yell but couldn't make a sound. Wyatt turned around and swam back toward Yindi and I, as Toba hollered and shouted and climbed lower to smack the surface of the water with the palm of his hand— *smack, smack, smack, smack!*

Frantic, Yindi climbed down right were she stood and yelled to Wyatt. I was afraid she would slip and fall in, too. "Swim to me, Wyatt!" she shouted. "Hurry!"

I stepped from one rock to the next, short of breath and nearly hysterical, trying to get to Yindi as fast as I could.

Wyatt made it to her and reached out his arm as the croc inched ever closer. Yindi was in a precarious position. Water flowed over the top of her head. Her footing wasn't stable. I finally made it to her and knelt down behind a rock in the shallows. Water flowed around me as I leaned over and took hold of the back of Yindi's shirt so she wouldn't be knocked over by the force of the falls. When I looked into the water below, the croc was nowhere to be seen.

Toba was still slapping the water's surface with his palm—*smack, smack, smack*! Maybe he had scared it away!

Yindi took Wyatt's hand and hoisted him up. He put one foot on a rock, and with his free hand reached through the falls and found a solid hold, pulling himself higher. He was completely out of the river, but only by inches.

"Come on, Wyatt. A little higher!" I was thinking, as he reached through the falls, searching for his next hold. A couple feet up, he found one, and pulled at it to make sure the hold was secure. It was.

"I'll move up higher so you can step here!" Yindi shouted over the sound of rushing water.

Yindi climbed back to the top of the falls, while I kept ahold of her shirt. As Wyatt waited, he and I made eye contact. The look he had was one of overwhelming relief. The thought even crossed my mind that one day we might all laugh like crazy about this!

When Yindi was safely seated on the rock ledge, I let go of her shirt and turned to my brother. He was testing another hold, and was just about to take his next step, when a croc the size of a dinosaur shot out of the water and locked its jaws on the back of his leg!

Wyatt screamed and I grabbed him around the back of the neck! The croc thrashed its head backward, tearing the bottom leg of Wyatt's pants right off. Fortunately, his leg wasn't in the croc's mouth, too. It was still attached to his body!

Wyatt was crying out, "Pull me up! Pull me up!" and I did, by his head, with the help of Yindi, who had a hold of his belt. I'm telling you, I was pulling so hard I'm surprised I didn't rip his head right off, but Wyatt didn't seem to care. He was back atop the rock crossing, high above the river and out of harms way.

We couldn't catch our breath, much less speak. We all lay there on the rocks, the water moving around us and cascading over the falls.

When Toba made his way back to us, he was practically dancing with delight.

"Talk about a dramatic escape, eh?" he said. "I've never seen anything like that in all my life! Whoo-hoo! Sorry big boy!" he yelled to the crocodile. "Oh-no, not today!"

Wyatt and I managed to roll over and take a look at the river below. The croc was still there, floating a few feet from the waterfall, the leg of Wyatt's pants hanging from its mouth. Toba wasn't exaggerating. He was a big boy. Somewhere between 16 and 18 feet long, I'd guess.

Toba continued to dance, almost taunting the croc, which I think made it mad, because all of a sudden the croc opened its mouth and hissed. This made Toba hoot and holler even louder.

"No, no, no, big boy! Not today! Ha-ha-ha!"

Wyatt and I looked at one another and smiled.

"You know, Toba," I said. "It might be a little too soon to heckle the croc. We still haven't made it all the way across."

"Hop on my back, Wyatt," Toba said. "I will carry you and Yindi can carry your backpack."

It was a kind offer, but Wyatt was determined to do it on his own.

"Thank you," he said, "but I can make it myself."

"Fine by me. Just be extra careful this time, yeah?"

"Trust me, I will."

Wyatt was extra, extra careful! We all were. There wasn't room for the slightest error because that big old croc followed us every step of the way, floating along beneath us as we moved, just hoping one of us would stumble so that he could fill that big belly of his.

The remainder of the crossing, because we had a croc following us and all, seemed to take forever and a day. Finally, though, we arrived at the far side where there was a low cliff that was dry and easy to climb. Standing atop the flat rock, looking down at the crocodile some 30 feet below, I noticed that my legs were shaking like a leaf. I sat on a rock, to rest my legs, and caught sight of my brother's face. He didn't look so good. His eyes were glassed over and he had a far-off gaze, like he was in shock. I smacked him on the shoulder, hoping to snap him out of it.

"Hey, you okay, bro?" I asked.

An uneven grin spread across his face.

"Never been better," he said.

At that, his eyelids fluttered and he collapsed to the ground like a cooked noodle, completely drained of all energy.

He's okay now, but to be safe, we're giving him some time to recoup in the shade before we make the final push to the village. The distance is not much farther. Toba says a couple hours tops.

WYATT

MARCH 20, 4:26 PM
ARNHEM LAND, VILLAGE
97° FAHRENHEIT, 36° CELSIUS
WIND: 0-5 MPH

We made our way into the village looking like a band of ragged outlaws. As we walked along the dirt road past small homes, people watched us with wary eyes. Or it could have been that they knew of the plane crash and their looks were that of astonishment. Maybe to them we looked like ghosts that had risen from the dead.

Toba and Yindi introduced us to Jarli and explained who we were. The old man had a big, bushy white beard, crazy white hair like Einstein's and wore silver rimmed sunglasses. Behind the dark shades, Jarli's eyes looked us over.

After a moment, he shook his head thoughtfully.

"Was this the purpose of your walkabout?" he asked his grandchildren. "To go looking for the people who were in the plane crash?"

"Yes, it was," Yindi said. "We knew that if there were survivors, they would need our help."

Jarli patted them on the shoulders.

"I am very proud," he said. "You have done a very brave thing. As for you two young men." Jarli stopped, pulling at his beard with his fingers. "I assume you do not have a permit to be in Arnhem Land."

"I'm sorry, sir, we don't," I said, unable to look him in the eyes.

"Visits here are highly regulated and our rules are strictly enforced," he continued. "We do this to protect our environment and ceremonial grounds."

"We understand," Gannon said timidly. "And we're sorry."

Jarli took off his sunglasses and held them at his side, all the while staring at us with narrow, scornful eyes. I swallowed hard, not knowing what to say. Submitting to the power of his gaze, my head dropped and I looked to the ground.

"I suppose no one ever expects that their plane will crash, now do they?" he said.

I looked up and met Jarli's eyes. A smile had come over his face.

"No, sir," I said, relieved.

"I am just happy to see that you are both alive and well."

We went on to explain to Jarli that Pete was missing and to ask if he had heard anything about him. Jarli had not, and called on Toba and Yindi's father, Daniel, to radio the nearby outstations to see if anyone had turned up.

While we wait for news, we've met several of Toba and Yindi's relatives and friends. Everyone here has been very welcoming and helpful, feeding us a delicious meal, and offering us a place to clean up and wash our clothes. Jarli's wife, Biralee, even mixed a remedy for our sunburns and bug bites.

"Oh my gosh, the relief!" Gannon said, as he slathered the remedy over his welted and parched skin. "What's this paste made of?"

"Ground up witchetty grub," Biralee said.

"What's that?"

"A big white larva."

Gannon paused.

"You mean, like maggots?" he asked.

"Mmm-hmm."

"Ooo-kay then," Gannon said, setting the bowl of witchetty aside and wiping the rest of the paste from his hands. "Probably shouldn't have asked."

"Agree," I said. "All that matters is that it works."

We quickly finished our treatment, cleaned ourselves of the witchetty grub and are now resting on the porch of Jarli's home, still awaiting any word on Pete. Daniel is also putting out calls to see if he can help us track down our parents. I am so anxious to talk to them I can hardly stand it.

GANNON
5:11 PM

News just came over the radio.

Yesterday, an unidentified man was found about a half day's hike from here and was taken to a village about 20 kilometers away. He was discovered at the base of a rocky escarpment with a broken leg and no memory of what had happened. He did not even know his own name.

"That has to be Pete," I said.

"I hope it is," Wyatt said. "But how can we be sure?"

Daniel had reached out via radio to friends who work for Outback Rescue. We asked if he could relay a few questions.

He pressed a button and spoke into the transmitter.

"The boys Toba and Yindi found asked if the man you rescued has brown hair, brown eyes, and a three- to four-inch cut on the left side of his forehead."

Daniel let go of the button and listened. I gnawed on my lip fearfully as we awaited a response.

"Affirmative," a man said. "Fits the description perfectly. Do the boys know this man's name? He's doing better, but still doesn't remember much."

"Yes, we do," I said.

Daniel handed me the radio transmitter. I pressed the button and spoke into it. "His name is Peter Campbell. He's a pilot from Darwin. We were with him on the way to the koala preserve when our Cessna engine blew up and we crashed." I turned to Wyatt. "When was that, a couple weeks ago?"

"Five days ago," Wyatt said.

"Jeez, seems like so much longer! Okay, the crash was five days ago. Pete suffered a concussion and we set up a camp so he could rest, but he wandered off and we couldn't find him."

"He should have stayed in camp," the man said. "He ended up with a broken leg when he fell from a cliff. Lucky he wasn't killed. If the rescue team hadn't found him the animals would have finished him off before morning."

"Is he going to be okay?" I asked.

"It is going to take some time for his brain to heal, but we have seen injuries like this before and are fairly certain he'll recover fully."

"Oh, jeez, is that great news!" I said.

Truth is, it's even better than great news. I'd go as far as to call it a miracle. It makes me happy just thinking about it. Good old Pete, alive and well. Okay, maybe not so *well*, but alive and on the road to recovery.

WYATT

MARCH 20, 7:41 PM
ARNHEM LAND
93° FAHRENHEIT, 34° CELSIUS
WIND: CALM

Daniel finally tracked down my dad in Jabiru. They had recently arrived and were preparing to join the search. After learning that we were safe my mom was so grateful she fell to pieces, crying and crying until she literally wore herself out. I'm guessing she's probably in a mild state of shock.

My dad took our radio call from the Outback Rescue office.

"You have no idea what your mom and I have gone through over the past couple days," he told me over the radio.

"I'm sorry, Dad."

"It's not your fault. We knew you had the strength and smarts to survive out there, we did, but that only mattered if you had both been lucky enough to survive the plane crash." My dad's voice cracked. "Well, with no mayday calls or contact of any kind, survival didn't seem likely . . ." He couldn't go on.

"It was killing us that we couldn't reach you," I said. "The radio was knocked out when the engine exploded."

"The engine exploded?" my dad gasped.

"It did. And wait until you hear about the snakes, dingoes, and crocs. Oh, and my unsuccessful kangaroo hunt!"

"I can't wait to hear all about it. Where's Gannon? How's he doing?"

"He's off napping," I said. "I'll be honest, he went through a rough patch out there, but he's regained most of his strength and should be fine. I'll have him reach out to you as soon as he's awake."

"That would be great."

"This may sound odd, Dad, but there was definitely an upside to being stranded in the Outback."

"And what was that?"

"Without a doubt, it made for one of the best research expeditions we've ever been on."

My dad gave a surprised laugh.

"Leave it to you to find the silver lining," he said.

"Now that we're safe, it's easy to look at the bright side. A couple of days ago, I wasn't so optimistic. I really thought our time was up. Anyway, you can read all about it in our journals."

"Your mom and I will do that soon. Listen, we can meet you tomorrow in the village or in Alice Springs. We just need to arrange transportation to one or the other. What would be best?"

"Let me find out if there's a way we can get to Alice Springs. Then we can all meet there."

"Okay."

"You know, Dad, I really think we need to finish off our adventure as planned. It's like Gannon said, we've come all this way, we can't leave without seeing Uluru!"

"He's right. We'll resume the itinerary as scheduled."

"Great, thanks, Dad."

"Hey, Wyatt."

"Yeah, Dad?"

He paused to gather himself.

"Your mom and I love you and Gannon," he said, his voice cracking again. "We love you very, very much."

"We love you too, Dad. Please give Mom the biggest hug ever from us."

"I'll do that."

I set the radio down, thanked Daniel and walked back toward the village, wiping tears from my eyes as I went.

GANNON
POST JAM SESSION AND DREAMTIME LESSON

Okay, not to brag or anything, but I totally rock at the didgeridoo!

I'm serious, if a career in filmmaking doesn't work out, I'm starting a band with yours truly on lead vocals and didg! That's what they call it here, the *didg* (pronounced "dij").

Heck, I'm such a good brother, I'll even let Wyatt join my band despite the fact that he has no musical talent whatsoever. He can stand in the background and hum or snap his fingers or something. We'll call ourselves G-Man and the Indigenous Melodies and write songs that are influenced by different types of music from all around the world. Oh, man, I'm totally digging this idea!

My inspiration for the band came early this morning when Yindi asked if we'd like to join Jarli and Toba on a short trek to find wood. After making sure we wouldn't be imposing, Wyatt and I accepted the invitation and soon after followed them into the forest. After a short walk, Jarli stopped to inspect several trees.

"What's he doing?" I asked.

"These are yiḏaki trees," Toba said. "Jarli's looking for a dead tree that's been hollowed out inside by termites. These are the trees we use to make a didgeridoo."

Jarli would step to the dead tree and tap it with his knuckle. If it made the right sound, he could tell it had been cleared out by termites. When he found a good, hollow tree, he'd give a nod and Toba would chop it down at the base. The tree trunks were maybe six to seven feet in length and about as big around as a grapefruit. Each of us carried back two trunks to the village.

There, we settled in Jarli's workshop and he showed us how to turn this dead tree into a musical instrument, smoothing out the hollow inside with a long, skinny blade and then carefully covering the top of one side with melted beeswax to form a mouthpiece before it dries.

Making a didgeridoo the right way takes lots of practice, patience, and expertise. It has to be cut and shaped just so, or else it won't sound right. After observing the skill with which Jarli carved the instrument, I had serious doubts that I could actually do it myself, at least not on the first try. As for playing it, though, it's like I said, I totally rock! Again, I'm not trying to boast, it's just a fact. Even Jarli was impressed.

"Have you ever had any training, Gannon?" he asked.

"To tell you the truth, Jarli," I said, "I've never even held a didgeridoo until today."

"I am amazed that you picked it up so quickly."

"All I had to do is study your techniques. You're the master!"

Jarli smiled and gave me some more pointers, telling me to keep my lips loose and just blow air through them so that they flutter and vibrate. What was harder to pick up on was how he changed the sound.

"The sound originates in your lungs," Jarli said, "and can be changed by moving the muscles in your throat."

"Can I give it a try?" Wyatt asked.

"Please do," he said, and gestured to his grandson, who carried a didgeridoo to Wyatt.

Wyatt put the didgeridoo to his lips and blew. I can't say I was expecting much, but Wyatt's didgeridoo playing was about as charming as a camel breaking wind.

All the didgeridoo music, along with the recent heroics of Toba and Yindi, who were very much the talk of the town, had everyone in somewhat of a festive mood, inspiring Jarli to arrange a traditional dance. Several Aboriginal men painted themselves in red and white ochre and acted out an ancient story about the hunting of emu. Wyatt asked permission and, once granted, took a few photographs.

Before night's end, Jarli was kind enough to explain a little bit about the Aboriginal Dreamtime and songlines. He said that it would be nearly impossible for Wyatt and I to comprehend it completely. According to Jarli, as outsiders we have a different view of life, a different reality, and that's why it's difficult to make sense of their stories.

"We are the first people," Jarli said. "Our creation stories, or songlines, are always evolving. We continue to create the world through our Dreamtime, walking and singing creation into existence. A song may begin here in the Top End of Australia and carry all the way to the southern coast, through many different tribes. As it travels, it creates all that we see."

"So there are songlines crisscrossing Australia?" I asked.

"The songlines not only crisscross the land, they are the land."

Wow, that's fascinating, I was thinking to myself, even though I didn't totally get it.

"Can we see these songlines?" I asked.

"We can, you can't," Jarli said with a smile. "It is difficult to explain. This is just the way it is. Maybe the bigger idea, the takeaway for you, is that the land means everything to us. The land has always provided for us. Our ancestors created it with their songs and they are all still very much a part of it, too. In other words, our ancestors, they are still here. The land, it is sacred."

"Now that, I understand," I said. "Well, most of it, at least."

Here's the thing: the wisdom of the indigenous cultures, like the Aboriginal idea of the land being sacred and preserving it for future generations, isn't always taught in schools. All the more reason to make it my mission to spread these ideas to as many young people as I can. Aboriginals would no sooner harm the land than they would throw themselves off a cliff. Many people today have a completely different view of nature and the environment than Aboriginals do. I'm not saying one is right and one is wrong. It's a lot more complicated than that. It's like I told Wyatt earlier on in our expedition, I simply think we can do ourselves and the planet some good by learning more about how certain indigenous cultures live in harmony with nature.

I have to say, this has been one of those totally epic, memorable, and mind-blowing kind of days. I mean, for starters, no one got eaten by a croc, we made some great new friends, and even though he's banged up pretty good, Pete is alive! We also heard that Darla and Roman are on their way to the outstation where he's recovering. Tomorrow, the Royal Flying Doctors, a group that provides emergency medical service in the remote Outback, are transporting Pete to Alice Springs where he'll see a doctor who specializes in treating patients with head trauma, just to make sure his recovery goes as well as it can. Since there are extra seats on the plane, Jarli asked if they could give Wyatt and me a lift. Out of respect for Jarli, and probably as a courtesy given all we've been through, they agreed, so we'll get to reunite with everyone tomorrow. Best of all, my parents will be waiting at the airport to pick us up!

An Aboriginal dance

WYATT

Our parting today was a tough one.

On our way to the jeep, we found Toba and Yindi and all wrapped one another in a giant group hug. Without them, Gannon and I would not have survived. It's that simple. For their kind and brave act, we will forever be in debt.

"Before you go," Yindi said, "I have something for you."

Yindi removed a rolled up canvas from her satchel. Shyly, she handed it to me.

"I made it for you and Gannon," she said.

I took the canvas and unrolled it. Painted on the inside were wide flowing patterns of blue, like a snake or a river, and several green and gray circles with smaller circles inside each. Decorating much of the canvas were bright white and red dots.

"You painted this, Yindi?" I asked.

"I did," she said humbly. "This is the story of Toba and I finding you and your brother," she said. "See here, these green, blue, and red patterns represent the trees, rocks, rivers, and billabongs. The white dots that weave through the colors, that is the path we took to find you and bring you back across the river to safety."

"It's beautiful," I said.

"I had no idea you were such a talented artist," Gannon said.

"What a special gift, Yindi. Thank you."

"Honestly, we'll cherish it forever."

Yindi smiled shyly. Toba did, as well.

"I guess this is goodbye," she said.

"I guess so," Gannon said. "But I promise you this, as long as we live, we'll never forget you."

Again, we all hugged.

"You two stay out of trouble," Toba said.

"We'll do our best," Gannon said, with a sly grin.

Jarli honked the horn of the jeep. It was time to drive to the outstation, reunite briefly with Darla and Roman, and catch Pete's medical evacuation flight to Alice Springs.

"The old man will leave you if you don't hurry," Toba said.

We turned, ran to the jeep and hopped inside. Jarli shifted gears and sped off.

"Bye Gannon and Wyatt!" Yindi shouted, waving as the jeep drove away. We both turned and waved back to our friends, watching them grow smaller and finally disappear behind a cloud of dust.

The drive was bumpy along the dirt road. We sped past a few old cabins, an abandoned gas station, and another station, further along, that was open for business. But mostly we were surrounded by more of the untouched, sacred Outback landscape.

When we arrived at the landing strip, Jarli helped us unload our gear. After checking to make sure we had everything, he brought us together and placed one hand on my shoulder and one on Wyatt's.

"Next time you visit, and I hope that you will, let's make sure it is done the right way," he said. "You reach out to me first and we will all go on a spectacular tour of Arnhem Land. Bring your parents, too."

"Yes, sir," I said. "I know they'd enjoy that very much."

"I've been trying my best to not get all weepy today," Gannon said, sniffing, "but I'm really going to miss all of you."

"We will miss you, too," Jarli said with a smile.

"But, hey, we're going to take you up on that invitation. And when we do, what do you say we have another didgeridoo jam session?"

"I'm already looking forward to it," Jarli said with a chuckle.

He gave us each a firm handshake and ruffled our hair before jumping back in the jeep and speeding off.

As the jeep rounded the corner and was lost behind the trees, I stood there for a moment appreciating what a special family we'd just met.

Picking up our gear, we turned to an old, weathered hangar across the road. Darla and Roman were standing outside. Walking quickly toward one another, we met in another group hug. Gannon summed it up pretty well when he said: "Surviving a plane crash sure does bring out the love!"

"It's so good to see you both alive," Roman said with great excitement.

"Good to be alive!" Gannon replied.

"What you both taught us in Kakadu was invaluable," I said. "We wouldn't have survived without your knowledge."

Darla smiled modestly.

"I'm sorry we never got a chance to search for prehistoric fossils," she said. "I know that was one of the things you were looking forward to most."

"If Gannon and I have learned anything in our travels," I said, "it's that expeditions don't always go as planned. Besides, that's just one more reason for us to return."

"Great! During your next visit we'll go looking for the fossil of a Liasis dubudingala!"

"What is that?" I asked.

"Largest snake to ever slither on Australian soil. They were more than 30 feet long!"

"No offense to that species or anything," Gannon said, "but I sure am glad they aren't around anymore."

"Look," Roman said. "There's someone here who's excited to see you."

He pointed behind us, and we all turned around to see Pete being wheeled toward us on a stretcher.

"G'day mates!" he shouted with a smile. His leg was casted, and his face was scraped and bruised.

"You remember us, Pete?" I asked.

"Indeed I do! Little by little things are starting to come back to me!"

"You scared us half to death out there," Gannon said. "When you went missing, we didn't know what to do."

"I'm so sorry I wandered off, mates. Why I would have done such a thing I haven't the faintest idea. I suppose the knock to the noggin had me all goofy."

"We understand, Pete. Trust me, no hard feelings."

"I'm so glad to hear it," Pete said. "You two are good blokes."

The Royal Flying Doctors airplane, a white double prop, bigger than Pete's Cessna Caravan, with a red and blue stripe down the side, was waiting nearby. When the engines suddenly roared to life, a wave of apprehension washed over me.

"We better get going!" the pilot yelled. "Have to get Pete to the specialist!"

I looked to Gannon. Roman noticed our hesitation.

"Nervous?" Roman asked.

"Very," Gannon said.

"The Royal Flying Doctors are the best!" Darla said.

"It's true," Roman added. "They have an impeccable flying record."

Pete even chimed in.

"After our crash, you think I'd get in a plane with just anyone?" Pete shouted from his stretcher. "Hop on, we'll be fine. Besides, I'm ready to get myself into a comfy hospital bed and spend a little time in front of the telly. There's a cricket match on tonight that I don't want to miss. Australia's taking on Sri Lanka!"

"Okay, we trust you and all," Gannon said, "but just in case, are there parachutes aboard?"

"One for each of us," the pilot shouted as he climbed aboard.

"Well, all righty then, let's do this!"

Here, we said goodbye to Darla and Roman, just one more in a day of difficult departures. Though I hadn't known them long, I had become very fond of our new Australian friends and was sad to be leaving their company. I was also sad to be leaving the environment of Australia's "Top End" and wished I had more time to study the region's geological history, wildlife, and ecosystem. At the same time, Gannon and I were very ready to be reunited with our parents.

In spite of our nerves, we are now aboard. Midflight to be exact. I've been writing as a diversion, but to be perfectly honest, I will not be able to relax until we are safely on the ground. And now we have a little turbulence.

Putting away my journal.

Need to make an effort to calm myself.

Close eyes.

Deep breath in, deep breath out.

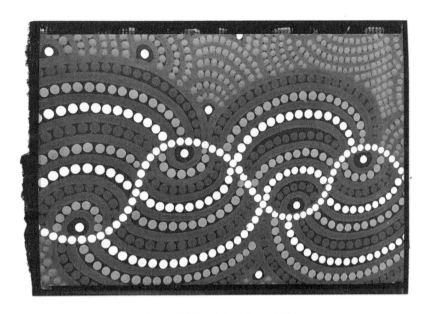

A beautiful Aboriginal dot painting

GANNON

You know, after being in a plane crash, my only wish was that the flight to Alice Springs would be a little less eventful, maybe even smooth, if I could be so picky. And it was, mostly, but it's never fun to be in a plane that has to land in high winds and, unfortunately, the afternoon heat had whipped up some serious desert gusts. As we descended, the plane wobbled back and forth, dipping and catching. This, of course, brought to mind our all too recent landing, which, of course, didn't go so well.

When the wheels finally touched the pavement, there was a loud screech. Or maybe that was Wyatt shrieking? I couldn't really tell. Anyway, I had a firm hold of the armrests as the plane bounced up, tilted abruptly, righted itself, and came back down, this time staying on the ground.

The pilot hit the brakes. The plane slowed. We were safe!

The propellers spun to a stop and we disembarked into the bright, hot afternoon. My parents, not having the patience to wait for us in the small airport terminal, came running across the tarmac in a full sprint. I don't know that I've ever been squeezed so hard.

"I'm never letting you boys go," my mom said, burying her head on my shoulder.

"You're going to have to," I said, "because I can't breathe."

"So this is what it would have felt like if that croc had crushed me in its jaws," Wyatt said, sounding like someone had tightened a vise around his chest.

My dad and mom let go of us and stepped back, their eyes wet with tears.

"Right, you mentioned something about crocs on the radio," my dad said.

"What else did I say on the radio, Dad?"

My dad thought for a second, then smiled.

"That mom and I could read all about it in your journals."

"You got it," Wyatt said, handing over his journal to our

mom. "It wasn't easy, but I think we documented just about every detail of our adventure."

She opened the journal and fanned the pages with her thumb.

"Wow, you filled every page," she said, and looked at Wyatt. "Come on, you have to tell us something. A preview, at least."

"It wouldn't be right to spoil the surprises," I interjected.

My mom and dad looked at one another.

"Fair enough," my mom said with a nod.

Just then a medic from the Royal Flying Doctors rolled Pete up next to us on his stretcher. We introduced him to our parents.

"Wonderful to meet you, Mom and Dad," Pete said. "You have some brave young men in these two. Brave young men, indeed."

My parents thanked Pete for the kind words.

"Well, I'm off to the hospital, mates," Pete said. "But before I go I just want to tell you how grateful I am for all you did for me after the crash."

"You would have done the same for us if we'd been hurt," I said.

"I'm just glad we all made it out alive," Wyatt said.

"I'll say!" Pete shouted happily. "Hey, how about we do it again sometime, yeah? Only without the plane crash and all!"

"We'd love to, Pete," I said. "Get well soon, okay?"

"Be good as new in a jiff, mates. Please stay in touch."

At that, Pete was wheeled to an ambulance and taken to see the neurologist at the hospital. I'm telling you, one of the hardest things about traveling is having to leave the new friends you make, and we've met some fantastic people here in Australia.

As for our family, we're traveling via jeep transport into the heart of the red desert where my dad has been painting since we left Sydney. Tomorrow morning we will wrap up this wild adventure with one of nature's most extraordinary spectacles, sunrise at Uluru!

GANNON

ULURU BABY!

Uluru, top elevation 1,143 feet

Okay, since Wyatt's already handed over his journal to my parents and "retired his pen" for the duration of our trip, I guess the responsibility falls on yours truly to write one last journal entry and bring a little closure to this adventure. And, hey, that's fine by me because this morning when I was in the presence of that massive red rock, a rock that seemed to have bubbled up from the depths of the earth, I was overcome with emotion and literally could not wait to write about it!

Watching sunrise at Uluru has to be one of the more magical experiences I've had in my life. What made it so magical was the way the early morning sun lit the underbelly of the low-lying wispy gray clouds like a pink and purple neon lamp; and the way Uluru, positioned perfectly between the low clouds, began to glow, like a river rock warming over a campfire, the sun turning it several different shades of red and orange.

People from all over the world come to witness this event and today Uluru did not disappoint. I saw countless photographers, Wyatt included, scurrying about for the best angle, snapping off dozens of photos, then racing to a different vantage point to repeat the process. I watched couples holding one another close, gazing at the rock in silence. I heard more than one person gasp. I even saw a woman dabbing tears from her eyes, this stunning sight obviously a bucket list experience for her. Maybe it's because my video camera was destroyed in the plane crash, but today all I wanted to do was stand next to my parents and take it in with my own eyes, to be in tune with the moment, to make a memory of it.

Some may have heard Uluru referred to as Ayers Rock. Well, it was never Ayers Rock to the Yankunytjatjara or the Pitjantjatjara people. They were here long before anyone else and are the true stewards of this land. So how did it come to be known as Ayers Rock?

I posed the question to my dad.

"Back in the late 1800s," he explained, "William Gosse, an English explorer, stumbled upon the rock and, ignoring the fact that there were people who had lived here for thousands of years and had probably already given it a name, called it Ayers Rock in honor of the former premier of South Australia, Sir Henry Ayers, a man who apparently never even saw the rock with his own eyes."

"Well, Mr. Gosse may have been a really important guy," I said, "but out of respect for the indigenous people, I'm going to call it Uluru."

"Good choice," my mom said.

After sunrise, the crowds dispersed and the tour busses departed, but we stayed around for a while, casually strolling the trails that circle the base of Uluru, mostly alone and enjoying that deep and heavy quiet that can only be experienced in the most remote places. That said, along the Lungkata path we were joined by a much welcomed walking companion, one of the most interesting creatures I have ever seen, the thorny devil.

The quick-footed thorny devil

We just finished eating lunch at the cultural center inside the park. It's a little past noon and I'm seated at a café table, alone and writing, while the rest of my family browses the museum. I'm telling you, there is a powerful energy around Uluru. Several times today, I've felt it moving through me, giving me goosebumps all over my body. It's a similar feeling to the one I had in Kakadu the night we camped on the rocks where ancient Aboriginal people once lived. One of the signs we passed on our walk today said that the details in the rock are the equivalent of sacred scripture. The features in the rocks tell stories. These stories are the cultural inheritance of the Aboriginal people and come with great responsibility.

There was another sign that read, "Look at the landscape as we do and know these ancestors are still here. This is the right place to learn about this story because it happened here at this place. Look, take note of what you see. Stop and read the signs, have a think and take in your surroundings. This is a place of great history, an important place."

Maybe that's what I'm feeling here, too. The presence of Aboriginal ancestors! I know it may sound strange to some, or even creepy, but to me the thought that the spirits of those who once lived here still roam this land, a land they loved and held sacred, well, that just makes me happy!

I'd have to say that this Outback expedition has only strengthened my admiration of indigenous cultures and their knowledge of the natural world. I'd also say, having had a near-death experience, it has brought me closer to understanding my own purpose in life, which is more than to just become a writer or filmmaker or whatever official title I may one day hold, but to focus my efforts, in whatever I do, on bringing young people together from all over the globe so that we might better understand one another, and better understand what we need to do, as a team, to help make the world a better place.

Okay, enough with all this philosophizing, if that's even the right word. We're off to visit a few local artists at a nearby studio and pick up the canvases my dad painted. It's almost hard to believe, but today marks the end of our Outback expedition. A few hours from now, we're catching the shuttle to the airport and flying back to Sydney where we'll over-night before making our way back to Colorado.

Listening to the radio this morning I heard a woman talking about the Great Barrier Reef. She was saying that it is the largest coral reef system in the world, stretches 1,600 miles, and contains something like 1,500 fish species. Hearing this just made me think, "Wow, is this country big!" I mean, you could literally spend a lifetime exploring Australia, and we've really only seen a small part of it. But, hey, as we told Roman, Darla, Toba, Yindi, Jarli, and Pete—one day, we shall return. All right, I better catch up with my family.

If I still had my Akubra hat, now would be the appropriate time to tip it and say, "G'day mates."

THE SIX ABORIGINAL SEASONS OF NORTHERN AUSTRALIA:

Gudjewg: December to March; hot, rainy, monsoon season; temperatures 24°–34°C

Banggerreng: April; knock 'em down storm season, as they call it; temperatures 23°–34°C

Yegge: May to mid-June; cooler, but still humid; temperatures 21°–33°C

Wurrgeng: Mid-June to mid-August; cold weather season; temperatures between 17°–32°C, so not sure why they call this "cold" weather season because those temps aren't very cold.

Gurrung: Mid-August to mid-October; hot, dry weather; temperatures 23°–37°C

Gunumeleng: Mid-October to late December; pre-monsoon storm season; temperatures 24°–37°C

Temperature conversion formulas:

$C° = (F° - 32) \times 5/9$
$F° = (C° \times 9/5) + 32$

GANNON & WYATT's

North Pole

The Alaskan Arctic

Greenland

Denali

Baffin Island

Kodiak Island

Cliffs of Moher, Ireland

Great Bear Rainforest

Niagara Falls

Stonehenge

Yellowstone Park

Paris, France

Moab   Badlands

Barcelona, Spain

Grand Canyon

New Orleans

Casablanca, Morocco

Tropic of Cancer

Everglades

Bermuda Triangle

Big Island, Hawaii

The Caribbean

Galapagos Islands

The Amazon River

Machu Picchu, Peru

Tropic of Capricorn

Patagonia

TRAVEL MAP

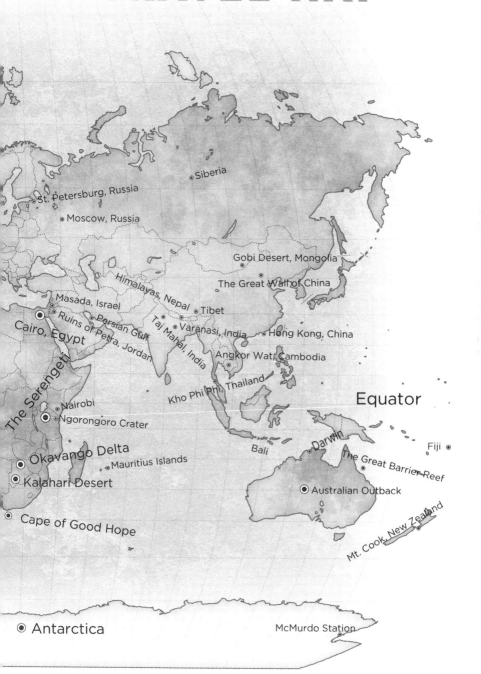

Siberia

St. Petersburg, Russia

Moscow, Russia

Gobi Desert, Mongolia

The Great Wall of China

Himalayas, Nepal

Masada, Israel

Tibet

Cairo, Egypt

Ruins of Petra, Jordan

Persian Gulf

Taj Mahal, India

Varanasi, India

Hong Kong, China

Angkor Wat, Cambodia

The Serengeti

Kho Phi Phi, Thailand

Equator

Nairobi

Ngorongoro Crater

Okavango Delta

Mauritius Islands

Bali

Darwin

Fiji

The Great Barrier Reef

Kalahari Desert

Australian Outback

Cape of Good Hope

Mt. Cook, New Zealand

Antarctica

McMurdo Station

MEET THE "REAL-LIFE" GANNON AND WYATT

Have you ever imagined traveling the world over? Fifteen-year-old twin brothers Gannon and Wyatt have done just that. With a flight attendant for a mom and an international businessman for a dad, the spirit of adventure has been nurtured in them since they were very young. When they got older, the globetrotting brothers had an idea—why not share all of the amazing things they've learned during their travels with other kids? The result is the book series, Travels with Gannon & Wyatt, a video web series, blog, photographs from all over the world, and much more. Furthering their mission, the brothers also cofounded the Youth Exploration Society (Y.E.S.), an organization of young people who are passionate about making the world a better place. Each Travels with Gannon & Wyatt book is loosely based on real-life travels. Gannon and Wyatt have actually been to Greenland and run dog sleds on the ice sheet. They have kissed the Blarney Stone in Ireland, investigated Mayan temples in Mexico, and explored the active volcanoes of Hawaii. During these "research missions," the authors, along with Gannon and Wyatt, often sit around the campfire collaborating on an adventures tale that sets two young explorers on a quest for the kind of knowledge you can't get from a textbook. We hope you enjoy the novels that were inspired by these fireside chats. As Gannon and Wyatt like to say, "The world is our classroom, and we're bringing you along."

HAPPY TRAVELS!

Want to become a member of the

Youth Exploration Society

just like Gannon and Wyatt?

Check out our website. That's where you'll learn how to become a member of the Youth Exploration Society, an organization of young people, like yourself, who love to travel and are interested in world geography, cultures, and wildlife.

The website also includes:
Cool facts about every country on earth, a gallery of the world's flags, a world map where you can learn about different cultures and wildlife, spectacular photos from all corners of the globe, and information about Y.E.S. programs.

BE SURE TO CHECK IT OUT!
WWW.YOUTHEXPLORATIONSOCIETY.ORG

ABOUT THE AUTHORS

PATTI WHEELER, producer of the web series *Travels with Gannon & Wyatt: Off the Beaten Path*, began traveling at a young age and has nurtured the spirit of adventure in her family ever since. For years it has been her goal to create children's books that instill the spirit of adventure in young people. The Youth Exploration Society and Travels with Gannon & Wyatt are the realization of her dream.

KEITH HEMSTREET is a writer and speaker who visits schools across the country to promote the importance of writing and literature. He attended Florida State University and received an MBA from Appalachian State University. Keith lives in Colorado with his wife and children.

Make sure to check out the first six books in our award-winning adventure series:

Botswana

Great Bear Rainforest

Egypt

Greenland

Ireland

Hawaii

Look for upcoming books from these and other exciting locations:

Iceland

American Southwest

Cuba

Don't forget to check out our website:

WWW.GANNONANDWYATT.COM

There you'll find complete episodes of our award-winning
web series shot on location with Gannon & Wyatt.

You'll also find a gallery with spectacular photographs
from Hawaii, Ireland, Greenland, Iceland, Egypt,
the Great Bear Rainforest, and Botswana.

And wait, one more thing . . .
Check us out on Twitter, Pinterest, and
make sure to "like" us on Facebook!
With your parents' permission, of course.

PRAISE FOR
TRAVELS WITH GANNON & WYATT

"Each of us has the responsibility to protect and enrich our community, to ensure that future generations inherit a healthy and vibrant planet. In each action-packed book, Travels with Gannon & Wyatt communicates these values and inspires young people to do their part to help make the world a better place."

—Robert F. Kennedy Jr.

"Wheeler and Hemstreet pack this slim adventure full of facts and trivia, as well as photos and drawings, lending it an educational slant. With clear nods to Indiana Jones and other adventure stories, the fast-paced plot and engaging characters are sure to appeal to a young audience."

—**Publishers Weekly**

"Simply wonderful books for young readers." —Dr. Wade Davis

"Travels with Gannon & Wyatt is a phenomenal series that encourages the next generation of conservationists to push their boundaries and challenge themselves to explore life outside their comfort zones. A must read for any young person interested in the wild world of nature that sustains us all."

—Brigitte Griswold, Director of Youth Programs,
The Nature Conservancy

"Twin teens explore various locations and introduce readers to the wonders, animals, and people of the places they visit. The books have a strong conservationist point of view, and the siblings encounter trouble not only from their natural surroundings but also from man-made threats to themselves and the environment. Each book also contains native people who help Gannon and Wyatt understand the areas they are exploring and, in some cases, help them survive . . . the books focus primarily on painting a picture of the boys' travels and surroundings, and they do this well. The novels offer good entry points into these exciting worlds and should be enjoyed by anyone who likes reading about adventure and discovery."

—School Library Journal

"Exceptionally well written and original, *Travels with Gannon and Wyatt: Greenland* is very highly recommended . . ."

—Midwest Book Review

"This is the brilliant first of what I hope will be many in a travel-novel series . . . Botswana has rarely had a portrayal that so accurately captures the physical and spiritual spirit of Africa."

—Sacramento Book Review

"This is a gripping novel featuring the land and culture of Greenland . . . packs a great deal of information into a short, suspenseful read that will appeal to fans of travel and adventure stories."

—School Library Journal

"Told in the boys' alternating journal entries, each of their voices takes a distinct shape: Wyatt is ambitious, serious, and clever (and he knows it), while Gannon plays practical jokes . . . Academic and enthralling, this book will entice fans of ancient Egypt and world travel."

—Foreword Reviews

"Gannon and Wyatt are a jet-setting pair of Hardy Boys-like brothers who solve mysteries while learning about different parts of the world. Along the way, readers encounter characters who offer information about the natural sciences and the history of Hawaii. The mystery plot makes a complete arc and includes plenty of detailed action scenes."

—School Library Journal

"I absolutely adore this series! Not only are there fabulous characters (based on a real set of twins who travel the world) but the gorgeous settings and adventures that Gannon and Wyatt face are fascinating."

—Heidi Grange, "Geo Librarian" Book Review Blog

"Young, would-be adventurers or armchair travelers will enjoy exploring with these two straightforward, engaging personalities—and will learn a lot in the process."

—Kirkus Discoveries

"Written in the grand tradition of the Hardy Boys, Tom Swift, and Willard Price's adventure-seeking brothers Hal and Roger Hunt."

—Michelle Mallette, Librarian and Blogger,
Shelf Life with Michelle

"Travels with Gannon & Wyatt is a groundbreaking series of adventurous stories like nothing else ever seen in children's literature."

—Mark Zeiler, Middle School Language Arts
Teacher, Orlando, Florida

"It's the best book I've ever read!" —Anna, 10

"*Travels with Gannon & Wyatt Botswana* is phenomenal! I read it in three hours!" —Felix, 9

"I just finished Hawaii and it was AWESOME! I loved how exciting it was!"

—Tai, 10

"I loved the first three books! Egypt was my favorite and I can't wait to read Greenland." —Kipp, 9

"A top-notch tale of adventure! Reading *Travels with Gannon & Wyatt Botswana* was like taking a journey into the heart of Africa."

—John Kingsley-Heath, Former Asst.
Director of Uganda's National Parks

MY JOURNAL NOTES

_____

_____

_____

_____

_____

_____

_____

_____

_____

_____

_____

_____

_____

_____

_____

_____

_____